For Betsy the Courageous

1

I wasn't sure who was more stunned, the twenty-two five-year-olds gripping their new Land's End and Pottery Barn lunchboxes or the parents who had started this whole fiasco in the first place. My daughter Nora stood between me and Jake, her little hands gripping ours, eyes wide as she took in the scene.

"You ready for this, kiddo?" Jake asked. He had to bend down to be heard. The camera my husband wore around his neck would have been entirely appropriate for a *National Geographic* assignment to document the annual migration of seals to the Arctic. When he stooped down to talk with Nora, the camera swung in a slow, heavy pendulum shift, nearly clocking a distraught blond boy clinging to a parental thigh nearby.

Nora didn't take her eyes off the scene, her first real day of big-girl kindergarten. She took in the blond clinger. Her eyes moved to a redhead busy using her rump to walk backwards and clear the field of competition to have the sand table to herself. She watched a mother who sat on a stool by the door and who was not just crying but weeping, including hiccups, as she pushed her unfortunate son to her chest.

I feared she had stopped blinking, she stared so hard and for so long. Finally, she spoke in an uncharacteristically small voice. "Not sure."

I crouched down, making myself eye level with my daughter. "Norie, honey, look at me."

She did. Her eyes seemed unusually blue this morning. Dark eyelashes framed her gaze and for some reason, the beauty of her face made the lump in my throat grow larger.

"Hey," I said, forcing a smile. "This is it! This is kindergarten! The land of big yellow buses and silly songs and writing with brand-new sharpened pencils and recess and"—I paused here—"and your own desk."

Nora cocked her head, and I could see a smile start to form. I was breaking through.

"You are totally ready for this." I marveled that I could sound that sure of myself when I was seriously considering scooping Nora into my arms, hip checking the clinger, turning over the sand table and body checking the hiccoughing weeper as we made a run for it.

Jake and his camera lens joined our little powwow. "Definitely, Bug. You were born ready. In fact," he leaned in and lowered his voice, "I'm pretty sure that by lunch, you're going to have to take over as principal of this outfit. These crazy people need a leader. I've seen *lots* of nose pickers in the last ten minutes."

Nora giggled. Nose picking for the win.

I searched the crowd for Nora's new teacher, Ms. Charm. I snorted a bit to think of that name again. When the introduction letter had arrived at our house, I'd snorted. When I'd shoved it into Jake's face the minute he got home, he'd snorted. And we'd snorted together on our way to orientation night, certain there was some explanation, certain the woman's name wasn't really, in real, adult life, the life away from coat hooks and miniature bathroom sinks, in that life her real name wasn't Calypso Charm, but call her Callie.

It was. It absolutely was. Her parents were free spirits, she'd said, and that apple had fallen awfully close to the tree.

I saw her moving through the crowd now, putting hands on shoulders to console parents and students, her smile brilliant, her mop of dark brown curls vibrating as she walked.

This time the snort was Jake's.

"Do you need a Kleenex, Daddy?" Nora asked, already rummaging in her stiff new backpack for the travel pack she'd tucked in an outside pocket.

"No, but I'm considering finding the nearest Catholic school and enrolling you posthaste," he said so only I could hear.

I nudged him with my elbow. "Remember orientation? Remember the phonics charts and the spelling lists and the addition flashcards? Ms. Charm might be wearing a hemp necklace, but deep down, she's a total traditionalist."

Jake narrowed his eyes before raising the zoom lens to his view. He snapped a photo of Calypso. "We'll see. I'm watching her."

"Ew. Don't watch her. Violating." I tugged the camera down to its Asian tourist position around his neck, though even Asian tourists had the decency to use their iPhones in close quarters.

"Good morning, families!" Ms. Charm's voice rang with startling cheer through the room. "Welcome to our first, fantastic day of kindergarten!" She tried to make us match her applause but we were having none of it. Not even Nora, the girl who had been plotting her escape to Real School ever since the disappointments of half-day preschool, not even she could be roused from her catatonic state.

"Kindergartners, I have a very important job for you, but this is a job only for children. Grown-ups are too clumsy with glitter so we will need to help them find their way to the hallway. Trust me, it's for the best. Can you help your moms and dads find their way to the classroom door?"

"Ooh, she's good," Jake said, a note of admiration creeping into his tone. He snapped one more photo of Charm, eyes still narrowed.

I pulled him down to me and Nora for an Elliott family hug. We squeezed until Nora laughed. When we pulled away, I blinked furiously.

"You're going to have a great day, Miss Glamorous Kindergartner," I said, pulling her to myself. I took a deep inhale of her strawberry-scented shampoo, felt her little arms tight around my neck, noticed the way she melted into me as I hugged her. Don't cry, don't cry, don't cry, I told myself. You will *not* hiccup. You are *not* a hiccup-er.

"Remember everything, okay?" I held her face in my hands. "I want a full report over dinner."

"Nose pickers included," Jake said, and he kissed Nora on her forehead. And then more quietly, "And if you smell anything weird, like a grassy odor? Or a strong perfume coming out of a burning stick? I want you to run to the office and call Daddy on his cell phone."

Nora looked to me for interpretation.

I shook my head. "Don't worry about it. Off to glitter. We grown-ups are horrible at glitter. You'd better take it from here."

Nora nodded. "I know you are. That's probably why you never let me do it at home."

I nodded as she walked away. "Right. Certainly not because glitter is of Satan."

Jake took my hand and we weaved through the remaining families. The Weeper looked like she might need IVs and a saline drip by the time this was all over.

"Wait! Mom! Dad!" Nora's voice preceded her as she darted among the lingering families. She reached us, eyes wild. Throwing her arms around our legs, she buried her face in our jeans. Jake and I leaned over in unison, covering her with our arms, holding her as she gripped us. When she pulled back, her eyes were shiny but she was smiling.

"Okay," she said. "You can go now. I love you!"

"I love you, too, sweetheart," I said, tears blurring the image of her as she skipped to the glitter table. Jake tightened his grip on my hand.

Nora looked back, one hand already on a bottle of purple glitter, and she called, "Do you know how to go home?" She pointed with her free hand to the classroom door.

Jake laughed softly. "Sure do, champ."

My smile was shaky. Of course we knew how to get home, but I knew as I walked out into the harsh sunlight outside Springdale Elementary School, home was going to look altogether different when I got there.

2

Jake and I sat on the porch, listening to the birds sing in the trees that arched over our street. The day after Labor Day, and already there was a delicious autumn crisp in the air. We sat in silence, and I turned around and around the image of my only child as I'd left her with a woman named after Caribbean dance music.

My only child. Well, maybe.

I turned. Jake, a man who lived in a constant state of motion, seemed lost in thought. He was staring at a sky spotted with billowing white. I took the chance to drink him in, feeling my heart constrict in my chest just like it had for all the years we had known and loved each other. I saw the jawline I liked to trace with my finger, the high cheekbones that I loved to kiss, the bright, searching blue eyes that I'd just seen reframed in Nora's face.

"What are you thinking about?" I finally asked. My voice was hushed, even in the quiet of the morning. I knew how difficult it was for me to leave Nora, and wondered what part of the good-bye had been toughest for Jake. Maybe he was thinking about the brevity of life, how fast our years were flying by, how it was just the other day when he'd emerged, sweating and victorious after installing Nora's infant car seat into the cramped back seat of our Honda Civic, and it was probably only going to feel like a matter of days before he was walking her down the aisle at her wedding.

I waited for his response.

He cleared his throat. "I'm thinking about how to max out our free airline miles on our Visa this year. It's going to be tricky now that we have to work around school breaks. Though we can always just take her out of school. You don't learn anything that crucial in kindergarten anyway, right?" He turned to me, earnest eyeballs, pondering the deep recesses of the universe, the passage of time, free commercial airfare.

I sighed. "Do you have time for a walk before you go back to work?"

Jake checked the hour on his phone. "Yep. Rob wants to go over Labor Day sales numbers at eleven, but I'm all yours until then." He wiggled his eyebrows in what I took to be a lecherous way.

I stared, willing my face to remain blank.

Jake sighed as he stood "But you want to *talk*. And *walk*. *Platonically*. For *miles*."

I laughed as I joined him. We turned onto our street and he continued in his tortured monologue, intermittently taking on his best therapist voice. "Because sometimes women need nonsexual touch from their spouses, Heidi. They need to feel listened to."

"Treasured," I added.

"Nurtured."

"Beloved." I was grinning.

"Why can't you feel all those things while you're wearing something skimpy and we are without a child in our own house for the first time in five years?"

I laughed. "I probably can. But first we need to talk. And plus, as you might have noticed, we are not exactly lacking in the fulfillment of marital responsibilities lately." Now it was my turn to raise lecherous brows.

"Heh," Jake said, a goofy smile on his face.

I felt relief to be talking about sex with a little levity as it had become a loaded topic in the previous two years. Jake and I had been trying for a baby with no success. That's not quite accurate. We had been trying to sustain a pregnancy with no success. We'd had plenty of help. We'd taken lots of time, the most common cure for most infertility. We'd been under the care of Dr. Kahn, my excellent OB/GYN. I'd taken a series of infertility meds to help my body remember what it did so effortlessly with Nora.

We'd gotten close. Six babies had made it to somewhere around the ten-week marker. None had made it past. Until now.

I took a deep breath and let the air out slowly as we made our way toward the park a few blocks south of our house. We walked without speaking. I watched the familiar houses roll by. The Greens' house practically shone in the morning light after a fresh white paint job done this summer. Mr. Green's oversized pots of red geraniums popped against the new color. As always, I felt the urge to climb the few steps up to their porch with a book and a cup of coffee. We passed Mrs. DeLario's tiny cottage, and I was fairly certain that if I opened the compact black door, I would find her sitting on her couch knitting and mid sentence about her no-good daughter-in-law who never visited, thank you very much. After we crossed the street and moved beyond the wild, last-gasp gardens of the VanKlompenbergs, tired sunflowers arching over a sprinkling of impatiens and new mums, we turned toward Our Park.

Our Park probably had a name. I'd never seen a sign and didn't really care to. Jake and I had called it Our Park since before we'd ended up buying a house in the neighborhood. We'd visited this park when we were dating, talking into the early morning hours while swinging long, slow arcs on the creaky metal swings. We'd walked to this park during the days right before our wedding when our mothers were driving us nuts with their power positioning about things like mints and the unity candle. We'd talked over a little wooden picnic table at this park while hammering out the details of the purchase offer for our first house, only steps away, full of charm and potential and an abundance of DIY projects, but *ours*. And we'd come to this park countless times with Nora, first just as a place to pace the stroller and beg her newborn self to cut us a break and take a nap. Then we graduated to holding her pudgy hand while she walked around the periphery and stopped to stare at the big kids and their rambunctious, life-sized play. And this summer we had visited this park at least twice a week and watched Nora face her fears and conquer the monkey bars, one bar at a time. She had proud calluses to prove she'd figured out how to go from one side to the other without pause.

Without needing to ask, Jake and I walked to a bench we favored that allowed us to look across the little lake to the far side of the park. We sat down and took in the water, the light reflecting off the surface and making the surrounding prairie grasses come alive as they moved in the breeze. We had the park to ourselves.

"Nobody's here," Jake said, looking around us, to the playground beyond.

I shook my head. "I got a flyer about a parent coffee in the school library after drop-off, so a lot of the usual park people are probably there, now that they are childless." I winced a bit at that word, hopeful Jake didn't notice. He hated it when I got pessimistic about our pregnancy quest, and I was pretty sure that included injecting meaning to words that didn't merit it.

Jake looked at me. "Didn't you want to go to the coffee? You could meet some school parents. Get them to tell you all the secrets, like how to steal doughnuts from the teachers' lounge and whether or not we really have to go to parent-teacher conferences in the era of e-mail?"

I looked at him out of the corner of my eye and sniffed. "You forget I already know all that stuff. Remember my life before Nora?"

Jake shook his head. "I sure don't remember mine. I think I used to have hobbies."

"When I was teaching, I was the master at finding the free food, including doughnuts, which typically showed up the last week of school when parents were wracked with sudden, violent guilt that they had completely ignored us the rest of the year. High school teachers' lounges aren't quite the cornucopias that elementary schools are."

I picked up a rock and skipped it onto the lake, watching it bouncing on the surface three times before disappearing. "And as for parent-teacher conferences, no one comes to parent-teacher conferences in high school. They assume if there's trouble, the principal will call. P-T conferences are so first-through-sixth grade."

"Listen, Eeyore," Jake said, "at least you didn't have to wear wooden apple necklaces. Or sing songs. Or have eerily perfect penmanship. You aren't mentioning the perks of high school teaching."

I laughed. "True enough."

Jake leaned forward, eyes on the lake, forearms propped on his knees. "Any regrets about turning down the offer to go back this fall?"

I shook my head slowly. "Not really. I'm glad I'll have the time to catch up on all the stuff around the house I've ignored for five years. And I'll be able to help Nora adjust to her new schedule without worrying about my own new, full school year."

The words hung around us, hugging us and doing their best to dispel the truth of why I hadn't gone back to teaching this fall. When the offer had come the previous winter to return to my spot as Spanish teacher at Springdale High School, Jake and I had both assumed we would have another baby in the house by fall. I'd even called my friend, Marisa, and cut out my hours working alongside her in her ESL tutoring service. At that point I was nine weeks along and heady with the knowledge that we'd never come that far, never made it to that point, and that surely this time was *the* time.

I'd miscarried the following week.

The wind picked up and pushed the shadow of a nearby weeping willow to move in ribbons over us. I shivered within my sweater.

"Jake, I'm pregnant."

He became very still, eyes fixed on the water. I saw his jaw tense, and then he spoke. "How many weeks?"

I knew it pained him not to jump up and down, take me in his arms, make me dance with him as he smiled and laughed at our good blessing. I knew it pained him because after the third positive test, he had done just that, again, and I had asked him never to do it again. It hurt too much with all our past failures, and I just couldn't handle that kind of unbridled joy in the face of potential heartbreak any more.

"Thirteen."

I heard him breathe in sharply. He turned, searched my face, his eyes bright. "That's really good, right? We've never made it to thirteen, right?"

I shook my head, a slow smile forming. "Not since Nora."

He bit his lip and I could see the effort he was having to make not to whoop it up. "What do we do now?" Hope filled his face and it made my heart fracture, again, with tiny, deep fissures.

"I have an appointment with Dr. Kahn this week," I said. I worried the cuff on my sweater.

Jake put his arm around me, pulled me to him. I hid my face in his neck, took in the goodness of him, the steadfastness of his optimism. "Thirteen," he said softly. "Thirteen is really, really good."

✦　✦　✦

I miscarried the next morning.

3

Maybe you've heard about the instinct for pregnant women to "nest." This is the phenomenon that merges hormones with the knowledge that a child will be descending upon one's home and that the presence of that child will likely require one to forgo things like toilet-bowl cleaning and baseboard dusting for the next eighteen years. So one cleans. With a vengeance.

A less acknowledged cousin of this condition is called *grief,* but the effects are the same.

It had been two weeks since I lost the baby, a turn of phrase that had always seemed particularly cruel, as if I'd been anxious to get to the food court in the mall or to my front row seat at the Bruce Springsteen concert and had simply misplaced the baby on the way. The thought angered me a little as I scrubbed the bottom shelf in a cabinet above the fridge. I was halfway through deep cleaning every cabinet in my kitchen. It was really astounding how much dirt could hide in the corners of your average kitchen cabinet. I pursed my lips and took to a back corner, arching my tiptoed feet as I stretched. I heard a percussive knock on the front door and a cheery, "Hello! Anybody home?"

"Here!" My voice sounded muffled from within the cabinet. I kept scrubbing, knowing that voice and knowing she wouldn't

13

mind.

"Wow. You're getting after it." A deep and masculine voice startled me so much, I bumped my head on the cabinet frame.

I withdrew my head from my cocoon, sweat on my brow and suddenly aware of my makeup-naked face. I turned and saw Annie (cheery hello voice) and her husband James (Deep Throat). James already had dark brown eyes that caused people to stare, but they had enlarged within the crime scene of my kitchen.

"You're a machine."

I decided to infer awe from his tone of voice. "Thanks. It all started this morning when I saw a dust bunny in the cabinet under the sink and, well, I guess it was time."

Annie was also wide-eyed, gathering in the piles of pantry food, pots and pans, trivets, flatware, and dry spices that littered the countertops and floor. She swallowed, appearing to take this in, this best friend from childhood and beyond who had morphed from the college roommate who regularly couldn't find two clean socks to the woman who stood on the kitchen chair before her. She lifted her gaze from a precarious stack of cutting boards and searched my face. "Heids."

The compassion in her eyes punctured something tight in my chest. The things I was guarding so carefully began to seep out from the puncture. I clenched my jaw, and I felt my eyes fill, but Annie was already pulling me gently down from the chair, folding me into herself. Strong, irritatingly skinny arms pulled me into a hug, and I stared at the ceiling, hot tears starting to stream down my face. We stood there awhile, and I could feel Annie crying with me. I'd spent so many tears in the last two years, I was always surprised that I could produce any more. Surely there was a cap on how much crying one human could do about one particular grief. Surely I was reaching that cap.

Annie spoke into my mess of frizzy hair. "Do you want to talk about it?"

I closed my eyes. I saw Jake lean down to kiss my forehead as they wheeled me in to the operating room. I remembered the weight of my body as it fell into a deep, blank sleep under harsh lights. I shivered to remember the hard, slow awakening in the recovery room, wanting to wake fully and be able to ask for more blankets, more blankets, more blankets. And knowing, too, on some level why I was trembling in a room alone and wanting just to go right back to that deep, blank sleep.

I shook my head. No, no, no. I did not want to talk about it. No more talking. I'd had years of talking, with Dr. Kahn, with Jake, with the endocrinologist, with Willow, my friend who prayed for me and my broken reproductive system. No more talking, thanks.

I pulled away from Annie's embrace, willing another makeshift patch over the puncture. I cleared my throat, looking at James, the Switzerland in the room. He stood with hands behind his back, watching the two of us while he bit his lower lip. I smiled at him. "James, I promise I used to be more fun before you met Annie in Italy and moved here from Boston and married her and made googly eyes at her all the time."

James made a face. "I don't make googly eyes. I'm an incredibly masculine black man. Incredibly masculine black men make smoldering eyes, not googly ones."

I laughed, the first time in days, I figured. One year into their marriage and I liked this man. It had taken me some time, all the adolescence in me rearing up when Annie returned from an extended stay in Europe with this James person, this James I didn't know and who had swept her off her feet and who maybe was secretly a video gamer who had emerged from his mother's basement to con a successful and beautiful dentist into liking him so he could steal all her money and dental instruments.

Turns out, James had enough of his own money and he was an above-average flosser as well. And he was absolutely smitten with Annie. So smitten that it made me a little nauseous at times, but I figured that was a fair price to pay to see your best friend so deliriously happy.

"Wait," I said, a sudden realization making me wince. "Isn't this anniversary week? What's the date? Oh, no, did I miss it?"

Annie was still wiping her eyes but was able to roll them. "Give me a break, Heidi. I have never, in all the years you and Jake have been married, remembered your anniversary. You don't need to remember ours."

"But it's the very first one. As matron of honor, a title that still disturbs me, by the way, I have *duties*. Matronly duties." I ticked them off with dirt-smudged fingers. "Hosting the bachelorette party, holding the bouquet during the ceremony, fussing with the train on your dress, making a toast at the reception. And remembering your anniversary. I should have sent you flowers or something!"

James produced a spray of daisies from behind his back. "Actually, we brought the flowers."

I reached out for them, feeling Annie go still as she watched me. I smiled. "I love daisies," I said, though she already knew. I buried my nose into the pleasantly bitter scent and tried not to feel like I was accepting a funereal wreath. "Thank you."

The front door banged open and Nora used four syllables to call my name. "Mooooooom!" She came careening into the kitchen and ran smack dab into James's legs.

"Hey, Sass," James said with mock offense. "Watch where

you're going, young lady!" He picked her up and turned her upside down. Nora squealed as she hung from her ankles. James pretended to ignore her as he greeted Jake. "Hey, Jake. Good to see you."

"You, too, James." Jake smiled and glanced at me. He had the habit now of checking on me whenever we were in the same room. The dark circles under his eyes were fading but the anxious glance was proving a hard habit to break. I buried my nose in the daisies again, glad for their distraction.

"I'd love to shake your hand but I'm a little busy right now," James said, keeping up the charade with Nora. Nora was nothing if not a good charade keeper-upper. She laughed so hard I was beginning to worry about upside-down vomit.

"All right, enough with the new guy. What about me?" Annie walked over to Nora and helped tug her to an upright position. She hugged Nora and looked at James with arched eyebrows. "Just remember I came first."

James performed a victory dance. I noted that his victory dances looked a bit smoother than my own.

"Mom!" Nora seemed to remember I was in the room. I took this as a positive step in our relationship. "Mom! Guess what we found after French toast?"

Jake and Nora had regular Saturday morning French-toast dates. For a couple of hours, I was left to my own devices and the two of them could conspire and chat and come home with something useless, bizarre, and/or broken that they found in the Goodwill store next to Opal's, the French-toast joint. Recent purchases included a crystal ball, a Napoleon Dynamite bobble-head, and my personal favorite, a fat stick of wood that had a ten-cent orange price tag attached. Jake had paid a dime for a fat stick. This was the kind of spell our daughter cast on him.

I sighed. "Oh, boy. I can't guess what you found. I'm nervous to guess what you found."

Nora furrowed her brow. "It's okay to feel nervous, Mom. That's your body saying you're trying something new."

Jake bit his lip, and I could feel Annie and James trying not to laugh. Sometimes Nora's parroting of my parenting made me sound a bit too much like a call-in radio show for my taste. "Right," I said, pulling Nora toward where I'd sat on the kitchen chair. "I'm ready. What did you find?"

Nora smiled big. "We found an *idea*. A Halloween idea."

I nodded, glancing at Jake, who looked a lot like the canary he'd swallowed was already in full digestion. "A Halloween idea. I pray it doesn't involve body paint and feathers like last year."

Nora dismissed this with a wave. "I don't even like turkey vultures any more. This year"—and she paused for effect—"Dad and I are going to be sparkly USA ninja warriors with leotards!"

"Leotard, *singular*," Jake cut in. "You'll be the only one who wears a leotard, kiddo."

Nora looked at Jake briefly, and there was pity on her face, which could have meant one of two things, either "Poor Daddy, he doesn't get a leotard," or "Poor Daddy, he thinks he's not going to have to wear a leotard."

"We have lots of pieces to get," Nora said, all business. "A sparkly skirt for me, sparkly shorts for Dad, headbands, wristbands, sparkle makeup, sparkly shoes—"

James elbowed Jake. "Dude, I'm hearing an emphasis on the sparkle."

Jake was starting to look concerned. "But Nora, remember how we talked about our sweet moves? How we can ring the doorbell and do some ninja warrior moves on the porches and do warrior jumps between houses?"

Nora looked in Jake's direction but didn't seem to register the words he was saying. She turned back to me. "I'm going to need some help with red lipstick. It has to be red. Everything is red, white, and blue. Because we are from America."

"Got it." I nodded. "I love you two ninja warriors. You're my favorite ninja warriors of all the ones I've ever known."

"Thank you," Nora said. Her little frame went into Jell-O mode as I hugged her and kissed her on her cheek, then her little neck, both spots a little sticky from maple syrup. The girl attacked her French toast with abandon.

After she wiggled out of my arms, she stood straight and cocked her head in surprise. "Mommy, what happened in our kitchen? This room is a complete disaster!"

Again with the parroting. It was becoming an issue.

"I'm scrubbing the cabinets," I said lightly, as if this were a completely natural sentence to come from my mouth. "And I'm pretty much done."

Jake cleared his throat.

"Almost pretty much," I corrected myself.

"We'll leave you to it," Annie said. She pecked me and Nora on the cheeks and gave a quick hug to Jake. "James has planned an adventure for us today." She went to him and looped her arms around his waist. "All I know is that it involves a picnic basket, a bottle of champagne and homemade scones. The rest is a mystery." She lifted her face and kissed him on the mouth.

I watched, feeling what anthropologists must feel when examining an artifact from ancient civilizations. I remembered, on a subconscious level, throwing myself headlong into moments with Jake. I was certain that had happened. It was just that the only image I could summon at the moment was the alarmingly large puddle of drool he'd left on his pillow that morning. Jake, too, had romanced me with baked goods this morning; he'd just bought the baked goods for our daughter so I could vacuum out dead bugs.

I waited, but just didn't feel the zing.

For his part, James was staring at Annie's face. Annie did, in fact, have a luminously beautiful face, but the silence left the other three of us in the room as three people too many.

I cleared my throat. "Googly."

James looked up, sheepish. "Sorry. I think we'd better go. Have a great weekend, guys." He shook hands with Jake and followed Annie to the front door.

We heard their muffled laughter through the windows as they walked to their car.

Nora ran out of the room, shouting something about the perfect blue sparkly socks she had in her drawer.

Jake leaned against the counter and crossed his arms. The body posture was casual, but I saw tension in his face.

"How are you?" he asked.

I knew this meant more than what it meant when he asked a customer coming through the door at his store or when he passed someone in the hallway in church or talked to Marv, our neighbor, over rakes and piles of leaves. He was asking how I was feeling, how today was greeting me, whether or not the coast was clear to tease and be light or if today was a dark day, one in which I needed to be alone and wouldn't want to be kissed or hugged or touched.

I breathed in, breathed out. I tried to take my emotional temperature but came up blank.

I shrugged. "I'm think I'm all right."

Jake's mouth pulled up into a half smile. "Would it help if I made googly eyes at you? My eyes can get really googly when the time is right."

I let out a quiet, exhale of a laugh. "Thanks for the offer. Still hitting me with new talents, all these years in." I pulled myself to standing and turned my back to resume work on the overhead cabinets.

I could feel Jake watching me for a while, our silence growing until the sound of my scrubbing drowned it out. I didn't even notice when he turned and walked away.

4

The thing about yoga pants is that you don't know what you're missing until you really commit to living in them for several weeks. I'm not saying the odd Saturday morning when you decide to read the paper for more than three minutes and try to remember what are, exactly, our three branches of government. I'm not talking about when you are woefully behind on laundry and have to wear yoga pants while you separate whites from darks simply because nothing else is clean. I'm talking about a full-blown fidelity to yoga pants, a decision to wear yoga pants and no other kind of pants for three weeks. This was the kind of vow I made and darn it, I kept it.

During Week Three, Jake and I were sitting on the couch late at night, watching a British mystery series set in the 1960s. The clothes, the beehives, the smoking—it all made me feel warm and happily detached from my own middle-class life in America, where Target was a stone's throw away, where melamine plates had won a definitive victory over china patterns, and where no one in Springdale had been murdered since the early 1900s, unlike this little English village where someone was done in at least once a week.

My yoga pants and I snuggled farther down under the quilt

I'd lugged to the couch as the final credits rolled.

"I totally missed that one," I said, slurping up the last spoonfuls of a big bowl of toasted almond fudge ice cream. "I thought the janitor did it. Who knew that professor was so nutty and disturbed?" I shook my head. "Never trust a man in an ascot."

Jake sat on the opposite end of the couch, chin in his hands. He seemed very far away. I stared at him while I sipped from a glass of water. Why did ice cream make a person so ridiculously thirsty? Was there a lot of salt in ice cream? I opened my mouth to ask Jake but he interrupted my thoughts.

"We need to move on." He turned his gaze from the TV. "We can't do this anymore."

I made a face. "Fine. I thought you liked the mysteries, but we can find another show. You tried to pretend you didn't like *Gilmore Girls*, but I think you secretly did. Like the episode when Kirk does an interpretive dance of his own birth?"

Jake rounded his shoulders. Eyes still on the television, he said, "I'm talking about us. Our sadness. We wear it like clothes, and I think we have to stop."

I bristled. "Grief isn't like that." My voice had a hard edge. "You can't just will it away."

He shook his head. "I'm not saying we can get rid of the grief. I'm not sure that ever really happens." His voice caught and we sat in a yawning silence. I felt my heart starting to race. This was exactly why I'd asked the yoga pants to be my constant companion, why the English vicar-turned-detective was such a good friend to me. I was tired of thinking about my empty uterus.

I didn't want to think.

I wanted to eat toasted almond fudge.

"I'm not trying to hurry us," Jake finally said. He turned to face me with a weary expression. "But we need to take the next baby step."

I narrowed my eyes at him, which was the opposite of making them googly. "First, I hate your pun. And second, what does that mean?"

He shrugged. "Go out of the house at night?"

"Geez," I said with a huff. "Fine. I didn't realize the TV-watching was such a raw topic for you."

Jake continued. "Go back to church."

I bit my lower lip. "Not sure if I'm ready for that. God feels like He's taken a road trip lately, and I'm not sure I want to track Him down."

Jake nodded. "Absolutely. But He can handle those feelings. We aren't the first and won't be the last to be angry with God."

I sighed. "What else, since it sounds like you've put some thought into this?"

Jake held my gaze. "We need to have sex."

Just in time, I swallowed my groan. "Not yet."

He shook his head. "Of course I won't pressure you or hurry you. I would hope you know that about me." His eyes flashed. "But I also will fight for us. The us we were and the us we have to become after . . . all this. And part of that fight is facing that we need to be together again, in every way. We're living in this house like roommates. And I hated all my roommates until you."

I slouched even farther into the couch. "That's just because I smell better and I wash my hair."

"It's that and a few other things." Jake moved to my side of the couch. He took both of my hands in his. "Heidi, I love you."

I nodded. The lump in my throat was making it difficult to speak. "I know you do. But I don't want to try for another baby. I can't do this anymore." Though I was saying those words out loud for the first time, I knew them to be completely true. "I'm just so tired. Feeling devastated makes me really tired."

Jake nodded slowly. "I agree. And Nora is noticing. She asked me the other day why you and I are never silly anymore." His voice caught again.

I shut my eyes against the sting. One more thing to feel guilty about. I couldn't carry a baby and I couldn't take good care of the baby I already had. My hand itched for the remote. I'd had enough.

Jake cleared his throat. "So I think we need to revisit the idea of Hope's Reach."

I stared at Jake. "Already?" I asked. "Isn't it too soon?"

Jake's eyes were gentle as he took in my face. "It's been two years, Heids. It's not too soon."

After the first year of trying, somewhere after the first several miscarriages, we'd discussed adoption. We weren't in the market for IVF, we'd decided early on. We'd accept minimally invasive help from my endocrinologist, but that was it. We'd keep trying, we decided, and then, after we felt we'd exhausted our options, maybe we'd adopt.

I'd never thought we would exhaust our options. Nora came so quickly, so effortlessly. I thought we would never have to circle back to adoption. The hypothetical wasn't dangerous at all.

Sitting on my couch, feet tucked under my legs and chilled even under the quilt, those early conversations might as well have meant the distance from me to Jupiter. But Jake's eyes held so much hope, such eagerness to hear me say yes, to say that we were ready to close this door of disappointment and aching and open a new one of promise and a fresh start.

I nodded before I could stop myself. "Okay. We can revisit."

Jake smiled, a teary, world-worn smile, but a real one nonetheless. He leaned over to kiss me gently. "We'll just look into it," he said, knowing his wife and that I needed to take lots and lots of small steps before taking any big ones. Jake, on the other hand, preferred acting well in advance of thinking. I knew it was a stretch for him to "just look into it," that he would much prefer to buy airline tickets that very night and think about all the other stuff later.

"While we're looking," he said, mischief in his eyes, "can we still have sex?"

I closed my eyes. "I suppose." I was smiling.

"And stop watching British period dramas?"

"Don't press your luck," I said and threw off my quilt. I padded to the kitchen for more ice cream before what I hoped would be a long, uninterrupted sleep. Moving on, I decided, was exhausting.

5

I knocked on the door to Nora's classroom and waited for a response. Knocked again. No response, but judging from the volume of young voices filtering through the heavy wood door, I suspected I would need to just go ahead and walk in unless I wanted to continue aging in the hallway while no one noticed.

I turned the worn-shiny brass handle and stepped over the threshold into the classroom. I stood for a moment, taking in what seemed to be utter mayhem. Twenty-six five-year-olds were busy doing all sorts of things, none of which looked like phonics. A group of them huddled around a cage that housed some kind of vermin. Another group was building with blocks, and the tower looked like it was going to fall at any moment, killing several children and one vermin. A third group sat poring over an oversized book and appeared to be engaged in a lively debate with lots of pointing at the open page. I located the petite Ms. Charm near the back of the room. She was holding up nine fingers and doing some sort of jig.

Honestly. It was a jig.

I walked into the room and caught Ms. Charm's eye. She clapped a hand to her forehead and made an exaggerated face of surprise.

Did I mention I used to teach high school? We weren't really into exaggerated facial expressions in high school. And we firmly opposed jigs.

I stepped over the debate team and made my way to Ms. Charm, already second-guessing my decision to volunteer in Nora's class once a week. After Jake and I talked, I decided that it was time to give the yoga pants a break. Just a sabbatical, I assured myself, but at least a few times a week when I put myself in the position where yoga pants would be socially unacceptable and where I could avoid thinking about things like all the due dates I was passing without needing to use the BabyGap onesies in the bottom drawer of my dresser. The tags were still on those onesies. The due dates came and went.

So. I needed a distraction. Or twenty-six. And my first stop was the classroom of anarchy led by Calypso Charm.

"Mom!" Nora spotted me just before I reached her teacher. "You're here!" She left her spot at the vermin viewing and came to tackle me with a hug.

"She's here!" Ms. Charm clapped and jumped up and down once in her clogs. "Thank you for coming, Heidi. I'm so happy you're here to help." She gestured widely to the classroom. "Welcome to our happy chaos!"

I took it in, forcing my mouth to pull into a smile. "It's great! Very lively." And by lively, I meant hive-inducing. The smile stayed put.

"Nora, would you like to help your mom get settled?" Ms. Charm said. "Can you show her our guest hook?"

"This way!" Nora said with no small amount of triumph. She took me by the hand and paraded me in a very indirect route through all the little bodies. I heard lots of awed whispers about my identity as Nora's mom. I was a pretty big deal in Room 12.

"You can hang your sweater here," Nora said, pointing at the first hook in a line of kid coats and lunch boxes. The hook was painted with stars and polka dots and had a cheery sign that read "Honored Guest." I shrugged out of my cardigan and hung it on the hook.

Nora pointed to the hook next to mine. "That's Gus Hill's hook. He had to pull a stop card yesterday." Nora shook her head and *tsk-tsk*ed like an elderly woman at a Miley Cyrus concert. "That was his third card. He has pulled *three cards.*"

In Nora's world, pulling three red cards from the cardboard stoplight on Ms. Charm's desk was just a little notch above being impeached from the presidency of the United States. Maybe on par.

"He's in my group for centers," Nora said. "That means he's in my group *right now.*" Nora looked at me like she was waiting for me to burst into tears.

So I was about to meet the famous Gus Hill. Gus was like a celebrity in our house. He was Nora's first encounter with a member of the willfully disobedient set. He was so notorious to her, she always used his first and last names together, presumably because that's how she typically heard them coming from Ms. Charm, as in:

"Gus Hill, please come to the front of the line."

"Gus Hill, your classmates are waiting for you to sit criss-cross-applesauce."

"Gus Hill, pull your third card and join me in a prayer you don't end up in a high-security prison."

That kind of thing.

I followed Nora back into the classroom. "I'm sure Gus Hill is just getting used to being a kindergartener," I said. "Some-times it takes awhile to learn all the rules."

We stepped around the reading group, now in a full-blown argument, and I thought of one of the high school students in my Spanish classes from years ago, a Gus Hill, version 1.0. Louis was an affable, friendly kid who didn't turn in one piece of homework or respond, even on the last day of school, to any question in Spanish. The most I ever got out of him was one day in the last quarter when I asked him, "*¿Cómo estás?*" and he said, "*Cerveza.*"

Lots of rules at school. Some kids were a little slower on the uptake.

When Nora had resumed her spot with the vermin and I returned to Ms. Charm's side, Calypso was busy laying out a line of glue pots on a semicircular table.

"This is so rad of you to come, Heidi," she said.

Rad? "Oh, it's no problem," I said. "Happy to help."

"I'm having a hard time getting parent volunteers this year." She shook her head. "I'm not sure why. People must just have lots of scheduling conflicts."

I nodded, wondering if it also had to do with Ms. Charm's parent-volunteer spiel she'd given on orientation night. First, she'd taken a full four minutes trying to locate the sign-up sheet before finally requesting that parents just e-mail her or send a note via her pet unicorn (Jake might have added that last detail in his later retelling). And when she explained what the responsibilities would be if a parent chose to volunteer in the classroom, I think she lost the first wave of prospective helpers when she mentioned "parent-initiated free writes." By the time she got to "parent-choreographed free dance," every eyeball was glazed over.

I'd e-mailed after my yoga pants divorce, but I'd made it clear I would not be available for tap or ballet. I needn't have worried, though, because Ms. Charm had responded, breathless, about her need for administrative work. She had a mountain of laminating and collating to be done, she'd said. Perfect. Stapling, stacking, cutting, pushing buttons: all of those tasks were perfect in my efforts to forget the hollowness in my body. Two hours of mindless clerical work and then I could head to lunch with my friend, Willow. Filling the hours, filling the hours.

"Just point me toward your mountain of paperwork, and I'll get started." I gathered a panoramic glance of the room, but there was more than one mountain.

"Paperwork?" Ms. Charm's forehead creased as she considered the word.

"You mentioned in your e-mail that you needed my help with administrative stuff." I smiled. "I taught school a long time ago, but I still dream about the laminating machine. Hopefully it won't attack me like in my dreams, but I think I'll remember how to use it."

Ms. Charm shook her head, as if to free it from so many confusing words. "Oh, no. I'm sorry. I might have said something about paperwork, but I'll always have paperwork. I'd much rather have you help me with manipulatives." She turned to face me and clasped her hands. "I'm so glad you were a teacher! You're going to be fab at this!"

"Well," I hedged, "I was a high school Spanish teacher. I didn't do anything very creative or interesting."

She laughed a tinny little laugh. "Nonsense! I'm sure you were inspired and life-giving."

Life-giving? Now she was making me sound like a placenta.

"So," she said, turning back to the table with the glue pots. "I'll have you take ten students here with you. The children can use the glue, markers, button, sequins, and feathers to create a portrait of Abraham Lincoln."

I stared at her, unblinking. "Abraham Lincoln."

She nodded. "We are in our freedom unit. We write about freedom, we dance about freedom, we made a mural last week about it. Lincoln fits right in."

Um, ¿cerveza?

Ms. Charm held up an outsized stapler and a large pair of scissors. Both items wore strips of yellow and black striped tape, reminding me of a police line. "These," Ms. Charm said in a deliberate tone, her eyes glued to mine, "are adult-only tools. No children can touch these tools. They are *dangerous* for children."

I looked around, hoping there was a child in the near proximity that was hearing this news for the first time, because certainly she was not talking to me. The only other adult in the room and a person who felt very comfortable with the inherent risks of office supplies.

She just kept staring so I responded. "Right. Adults only. Got it."

Ms. Charm, apparently satisfied with my level of comprehension, nodded and began dividing the students into three groups. Four of them marched to the front of the room to a small table where she said they'd work on their reading with her. A large mass moved to their desks to begin what Ms. Charm described as "independent processing," and which the veteran education linguist in me knew to be worksheets. And ten children skipped over to the Lincoln-in-sequins table with me.

I edged into the center of the semicircle and squatted down to the kid-sized chair provided, my knees pulled up to my chest. I felt ridiculous. One thing did come back to me, however, with more certainty than what I would have used to approach the laminating machine. All those eyes looking at me, waiting to see what would happen next, and I remembered the cardinal rule of teaching: to fake it was to make it.

"Hello, everyone," I said in what I hoped was a good kindergarten voice. I'd usually resorted to sarcasm and pop culture references with my high school students. The sarcasm was still alive and well, but I'd found Nora preferred literalism and I assumed her cohorts would do the same. As for pop culture references, I did not have one inkling as to what was happening in pop culture as a whole as I hadn't been to a movie since the time just prior to Nora's birth and the last CD I bought was, in fact, a CD. I did, however, know the world of Disney Junior and whichever animated character was on the current Chick-fil-A kids' meal. So while I had already caught myself daydreaming about ice cream and yoga pants, I squared my shoulders, trying to summon the energy I would need for life on the outside.

"What are we doing, Mom?" Nora asked. She'd run over to my table as soon as Ms. Charm had given her the thumbs-up, even though she was the only one from the vermin group to get a pass. She asked her question but looked at her classmates, as if to say, "This is my mother. I am the queen. Pledge your allegiance."

I opened my mouth to describe the Abraham Lincoln project, but a little boy on the end erupted in laughter. I looked to see what was so funny and saw him scooping up two popsicle sticks worth of glue from two separate pots and crossing them in the air, sending ribbons of glue over the table space between them.

"Gus Hill!" Nora's voice was loudest in the group's exclamation.

Ah. So this was Gus. He looked at me through round blue plastic frames, his smile poking two deep dimples in his face. He was adorable. And two steps away from pledging the fraternity known for naked romps through the quad.

"Gus, please put down the glue. We're not quite ready for that part yet."

Gus Hill put down the glue but reached for a tub of sequins. I swiped them out of his reach and launched into a quick description of our task.

"You guys remember Abraham Lincoln? Sixteenth president, led us through the Civil War, helped abolish slavery as an institution?"

A little girl in pigtails said, "Freedom," drawing out the word in two bored syllables. Her automaton response reminded me of how in Sunday school one always could defer to the perma-right answer, even if one didn't really hear the question because one was busy picking the glue out of the spines of the classroom Bibles. The answer, always and forever, was two syllables, drawn out and in a singsong voice: "Je-sus."

"Right," I said now, pushing down a very witty but sarcastic and therefore lost-on-my-audience remark. "Lincoln fought for freedom."

The pigtails girl looked pleased with herself even though, let's be honest, she hadn't exactly cracked the code on that one.

"So we're going to make a portrait of Abraham Lincoln using these markers, sequins, buttons, and, um, feathers." I extracted a fistful of feathers from Gus Hill's grip. "Let me know if you need help with anything."

They dove at the supplies like bottom feeders. Sequins and feathers mixed, every glue pot was turned over within seconds, and Gus Hill started using the end of a purple feather like a toothpick . . . in his neighbor's mouth. One little girl started crying when the boy next to her swiped the last pink marker out of the bin. I tried to console her by reminding her he wouldn't use it forever, but the word *forever* just made her cry harder. Pigtail Girl tapped me on the shoulder and asked if she could go potty and I might have snapped, "Whatever," before coming to myself and assuring her in a more syrupy voice that yes, she was allowed to go to the bathroom. Oh, for the days of high school students who just took the pass off my desk and went to the bathroom on their own! Sure, they spent an inordinate amount of time applying lip gloss and sneaking a smoke break, but at least they did those things without my assistance!

I glanced over to Ms. Charm, hoping for a little help, but she was fully engrossed with the group of students at her desk. She kept making a repetitive *t-t-t* sound with her mouth and seemed not at all interested in whatever consonants we were or were not using on the other side of the room.

"OWOWOWOWOW!"

I dropped the open container of sequins I was holding, Gus Hill's yelp was so loud and startling. I looked over to see him clutching his finger, fire hydrant tears shooting out of his eyes and down his cheeks.

"What happened?" I asked but saw the problem before the question was fully formed. Gus Hill had located the adults-only stapler, yellow stripes announcing its identity, and he had used that stapler to staple his finger. He held up the finger to show me. A mangled silver staple hung from his index finger, coated nicely in the blood that was making a steady trail out of his wound and down his finger.

Ms. Charm surprised me with her speed. "Oh, no!" She said, blanching slightly. If she was one of those people who passed out at the sight of blood, I was going to pitch a fit the likes of which these five-year-old amateurs had never seen.

35

Ms. Charm trembled a little while she held Gus's finger to inspect it. She straightened and seemed unsteady in her clogs. "Surya, please walk with Gus to the nurse's office. And please make sure Mrs. Hutchinson knows that a parent volunteer was helping Gus when this happened."

"I have no idea where he found that stapler," I said, and was ashamed to hear a tidge of whine in my voice.

Ms. Charm wasn't looking at me. She was sitting in the tiny chair I'd been scrunched up in before the bloodletting. She didn't even look comically large in it.

"I'd assumed I was clear about the adults-only issue," she muttered, wrapping a last Kleenex around Gus's wound before sending him off. "This is really so unfortunate because it was entirely preventable."

I made a face at Nora, hoping for some solidarity, and I got it. She shook her head in disgust at the Gus Hill phenomenon. Self-righteousness felt good.

"Heidi." Ms. Charm used the voice I assume she employed when reminding her class to use their inside voices. "Thank you so much for your willingness to help. I'll e-mail you if I have another time when we can fit you in."

Wait. I was doing this as a good deed, a way to make Calypso Unicorn's teaching life a little easier. Why did it feel like she was trying to do me a favor? Why was she siding with Gus Hill? He was a terror in Ralph Lauren frames!

I nodded and yes, yes, I did purse my lips. "Sounds good," I said, already scooting from behind the semicircular table. It was a challenge to look dignified when scooting.

Nora walked with me to the coat hooks, her face and gait solemn. "You didn't mean to make Gus Hill bleed, Mommy."

I rolled my eyes to the back of my head as I faced the wall to tug on my sweater. "No, honey, I didn't. Gus Hill made himself bleed, but it was accident."

Her lip trembled. "There was a lot of blood."

I crouched down to her eye level and pulled her into a hug. "I'm sorry that happened, lovey," I said into her ear. I could feel her little body fighting a sob. "Gus Hill's going to be fine. The nurse will clean out his cut and put a Band-Aid on and that will be it." Well, sort of, I thought ruefully. If you don't count the way the little Napoleon would enter triumphant, holding up his Ninja Turtle Band-Aid and playing the victim. Oh, the crippling of justice in the modern world!

"You okay?" I said, still holding Nora in a hug.

She nodded, sniffled. "Yes." She let go of me and wiped her face with her hands. My heart stopped a bit. I was washed in a sudden desire to take her out of school, rewind to every autumn before this one, when we had a long line of fresh days in front of us, ours for the playing and planning and cookie baking and park visiting or just sitting on the couch watching another Tinkerbell movie. I hated Tinkerbell movies. But what I wouldn't have given to pop a big bowl of popcorn right that second and sit down to *Secret of the Wings*. I swallowed a lump forming in my throat.

"It's almost first recess," Nora said. "I have to go." Then, as if she was reading my thoughts, she said, "Are you all right, Mama?"

I bit the inside of my bottom lip and forced a shaky smile. "I sure am, kiddo. And I love you so, so much." I pulled her into a last hug, determined to make it quick. Even so, I felt her wiggle free before I was ready to let go.

6

I met Willow at a new restaurant on Main Street. Willow owned her own art gallery and café, so it was something of an event to meet at another place for lunch. After twenty-odd years of making delicious meals for her friends and family, going out to lunch at a competing restaurant was not unlike removing Willow's toenails without anesthetic. She felt it was necessary to show support for other small business owners, and her desire for them to succeed was very genuine on a personal level. On a professional level, however, she'd learned it was best to take me along so she didn't end up giving her server a friendly twelve-point lecture on the Best Ways To Describe the Soup of the Day.

"I'm so glad you ask me to tag along to these outings," I said as we sat down at a table by the window. Juniper Row, the name of this new spot, was about half full at noon. "Not a bad turnout for the second week out," I noted, nodding at the tables around us.

Willow looked up from the menu, her eyes moving above the polka dot frames of her readers. "What? Oh, yes." She glanced at the dining room. "Not bad."

I cocked my head and stared at her. Same wild spray of curls.

Same beautiful, full face. Same billowy blouse paired with a long, printed skirt, a getup typical of a former hippie and a woman who had named her three children Hike, Blue, and Stream.

But there was something off.

"Willow," I said.

She kept her eyes on her menu. "Hmm?"

"You're being weird."

Her eyebrows arched but she still didn't look up. "I'm not sure what you mean.

I cleared my throat and gently pried the menu out of her hand.

"Let's review," I said. "When we saw each other outside, you stepped around a huge planter of mums and didn't remark on how the pink clashed with the red front door."

Willow looked nervous.

"When we entered the dining area, you didn't say a word about how dark it was and that black paint on the walls should only allowed in strip clubs."

Willow laughed and took a small sip from her sweating water glass.

"And when we sat down, you made not a peep about how the hostess was chewing gum. I'm talking a lot of gum. Hubba Bubba style, maybe two pieces. And she was smacking it."

Willow grimaced. "That's disgusting. Someone should tell her she is the face of the restaurant and the first impression guests get." She sat up straight in her chair, her head on a swivel, looking for Marcie the Wonder Chewer.

I narrowed my eyes at her, undeterred. "You're acting weirdsmobile. What's going on?"

Willow was saved by the approach of our server.

"Hello, ladies. My name is Boris and I'll be taking care of

you today."

Oh, dear. Two infractions already for Boris: He'd said he'd be *taking care* of us, a phrase that Willow always said brought the Mafia to mind, and he was laboring to crayon his name upside down on our paper table cloth. I tried catching Willow's eye to see the disdain settling there, but she was staring at her menu with a vacant smile.

"Can I bring you anything to drink other than water?" Boris was battling an acne problem, and he was so skinny, he needed to eat absolutely everything on the menu every single day if he was going to make it through another harsh Midwest winter. Since I was sitting with the Pleasant But Absent, I answered for both of us.

"She would like an iced tea, two slices of lemon, and I'll have a cup of hot tea. Mint, if you have it."

I waited until he rounded the corner before shaking my head. "Poor Boris. What a name. And the Clearasil issue can't be helping with the ladies, Russian or otherwise."

When I turned my attention back to Willow, she was flushed. Her eyes were shining and she was directing laser beam stares in my direction.

"Willow?" I leaned forward in my chair. "I'm starting to worry about a fever."

"I'm dating someone," she blurted, a bit loudly for what social convention demanded.

My eyebrows shot up to my hairline. "What? Who? How? Do I know him?" My mind raced. Had I seen this coming? I searched my mind for a blossoming friendship, a new romance, a particularly handsome UPS man. Nope. I came up empty. For his part, our Springdale UPS man had a bulbous nose and the tendency to snicker.

Willow swallowed hard, her eyes still doing the scarlet fever thing. "No," she said, drawing out the word. "I'm fairly certain you don't know him. He isn't from Springdale."

"Well, tell me everything!" I said. "I didn't even know you were looking to start dating."

"It's been five years since Michael died," she said, a little defensively, it seemed to me. "That's a long time."

"Yes, absolutely," I said, nodding. "You're young and should have someone in your life."

She made a face. "Actually, there's nothing like dating to make a girl feel very, very old. The last time I did this kind of thing I was able to go braless and barefoot without risk of injury to myself or others."

Poor Boris heard the "braless" part and had to scurry away from the table with a water pitcher his only salvation.

"Did you really not wear a bra? In public?"

Willow rolled her eyes. "Of course. I was ridiculously perky in those days, and I'm not referring to my winning personality. They were buoyant, these breasts of mine."

Boris looked at us from across the room, torn between his responsibility to take our order and his desire never to hear a woman in her fifties talking about her boobs. I shook my head, warning him that we were not ready to place our order and that the woman was not done talking about her boobs.

Willow continued. "Besides, bras are clearly a harness. They want to tie us in and keep us in line. They want to make us more manageable, less free to think for ourselves."

I furrowed my brow. "Are we talking about bras or Chairman Mao?"

Willow laughed. "Both. And I'm not so worried about either any more," she said with a shrug. "Turns out, as one's breasts start to sag southward, a bra is very practical."

Oh, Boris. Thought the coast was clear but just had to squeak in during the sag moment. He slumped into his bony shoulders.

"Are you ready to order?" he asked, sounding a bit like he was asking for last rites.

"Yes," I said brightly. "I'll have the Cubano, please."

Willow looked at her menu, her eyes scanning as if seeing it for the first time. "Oh. Um. I'm not very hungry. I'll have . . . this." She pointed. "The kale salad."

Boris scribbled and I felt my mouth drop open. When we were alone again, I said, "All right. Is this new mystery man a vegetable farmer or a cult leader? Which is it? Because my friend Willow hates kale. Despises it. Is prone to ranting about how people have jumped on a bandwagon of nasty, and that no one knows how to prepare kale well anyway, not like your friend from the Caribbean in '78 who braised it and served it on a coconut sauce with rice and jerk chicken."

Willow was giggling. "Wow. I need to get some new material. I didn't know I'd mentioned Adrian's kale that often."

My eyes were slits. "Vegetable farmer or cult leader?"

"Neither," she said, a smile already forming. "His name is Beau, and we've been dating for about a month."

"A month!" I said. I revisited all the times I'd seen her in the last four weeks and was astonished. "Willow! You sly dog!"

Her smile widened. "Well, I didn't want to say anything until I was sure there was potential. But now I know there is. Potential." Her eyes were sparkly, as in, the goal of Nora's life. Very, very sparkly and very, very beautiful. Happiness looked so good on her. I thought of all the tears, all the conversations of grappling with Michael's death after his long struggle with ALS, the battles of raising three teenaged boys alone, the fight to save enough money, enough time, enough energy to get them through high school and college. I felt my heart swell with relief. Willow had stayed the course, she had tirelessly worked for the next day conquered, the next day cleared, the grief to lift. I swallowed hard. So the grief did eventually lift.

"I'm so happy for you." I reached across the table and covered her hand with mine. "How did you meet? Oh!" I said, suddenly. "Was it at Makila Denhart's wedding? I saw you talking with that uncle." I wagged a finger at her. "He was cute! Wasn't he the one who races sled dogs? Or was that the actuary?"

Willow shook her head. "I didn't meet him at Makila's wedding." She fussed with her napkin, eyes down. "Actually, I met him online."

I stared at her for a moment and then, in a furtive attempt to keep from breaking the silence with my raucous laughter, I bit my bottom lip. Don't laugh, don't laugh, I repeated to myself. Didn't work. I laughed. Loud and hard. I shouldn't have, I know now, but it *erupted*, this laughter. I was at a loss to contain it. And not for the reasons you might expect, reasons involving online suitors having few other options or the meat-market atmosphere of Tinder or the way in which it begins, all secrecy and with a shroud of embarrassment.

No, I laughed because this was *Willow*.

"I'm sorry," I said through my final giggle. Willow frowned. "I promise I'm not laughing because you found him online. I'm laughing because"—dang it, one more bark of a laugh here—"because you hate technology! You hate cell phones and texting and DVRs and the World Wide Web, though you softened a bit when Al Gore had something to do with it. You hate computers! How did this happen?"

She shrugged. "I was talking with my cousin, who lives in Chicago, and she kept trying to set me up with all the divorced physicians from her country club. There are a lot of divorced physicians in Chicago, let me assure you. Most of them are bald, most of them love to golf, and most of them are divorced at least in part because they don't know how to be married and maintain their jobs at the same time. No, thank you, dear cousin." She sat up straight in her chair. "It was during one of her lectures on how I'm too young to shrivel up and die, alone and without one more orgasm before death."

I winced as Boris leaned over to deliver my sandwich. Boris was going to need to decompress after this lunch date. Maybe he would emotionally eat. That would be a win.

"I was listening to her drone on and on about how I needed to find someone, and I was saying again that I was completely content on my own and that if I did find someone, it would need to be someone from around here, when she started talking about her friend who had begun dating again recently after she divorced her physician husband." One of Willow's eyebrows arched as she went on. "And I learned about this thing called eHarmony." She said the word as if I would probably want to write it down, and would I like her to spell it for me?

"I've heard of eHarmony," I said, quelling my thirst for sarcasm. I'd also heard of Barack Obama, but I let that one slide.

"It's unbelievable," Willow said. Her eyes were wide. "It's so personalized. I don't understand the science behind it, but I answered a bunch of questions and real people, men with real brains, appeared in my in-box."

Willow had just used the word *in-box* in a sentence. I wished Boris had spiked my tea.

"I looked through all the profiles, of course," Willow said

between bites of kale, "but in the end, I only contacted Beau." She smiled at me. "Beau won."

I shook my head, more than a little stunned. "I can't wait to meet him. When can we all go to dinner?"

"How about next Friday? He'll be back in town after visiting his mother in Minneapolis."

"It's a date," I said, already entering it into my phone. "Where should we go?"

Willow shuddered. "Not here," she said. "It's too dark, the food is uninspired at best, and that Boris person wrote with crayons on our tablecloth. I'll give this place a month before it goes under." She looked thoughtful. "I'll need to remember to circle back and see if they want to sell the light fixtures. I do like the light fixtures."

I sighed, happy to see the world righted again. Willow was still Willow, and I couldn't wait to meet the man who had turned her head. Or her eyes to the screen, as it were. I stuffed a large bite of my sandwich into my mouth in an effort to subdue another giggle.

7

School had been in session for three weeks, and I could see no discernible difference between the total mayhem of the parking lot from Day Two to where I stood on the sidewalk that afternoon. We lived close enough to the school to walk and I had been impressed with the calm and orderly nature after the final bell at the end of Nora's first day of school. Waves of parents filed in and out of the front doors, chatting with children who looked rumpled and exhausted, peppering them with questions that, for the most part, elicited only one-word answers and a fair amount of whining. The parents were the picture of calm, and they absorbed the exhaustion and the whining along with bursts of pent-up energy while they walked leisurely to their cars, parked three abreast in the loading zone in front of the school. Some stopped to take photos of the kids on the playground, in front of the school sign, by the flagpole. Birds chirped, the sun shone.

That was Day One.

Day Two was Armageddon.

Gone were the niceties. Gone were the demure smiles and polite jostling of "After you!" "No, really, after you!" Gone was the slow amble back to the minivan, hand in hand with a child, the offer to carry the lunch box or the backpack.

In its place were Real-Life Mom and Dad. I stood on the front sidewalk, waiting for the final bell to ring and for Nora to come find me under our designated maple tree. I chastised myself yet again for failing to bring a snack or a lawn chair to take in what was transpiring like the entertainment it was. I knew that from my vantage point, I would witness children running alongside sensible heels like Chihuahuas chasing greyhounds, trying to keep up as their mothers raced out of the building and back to work or to soccer practice or to the junior high for another pickup procedure. I knew I'd see the dads with long strides finally tire of dragging their sons and daughters, the backpacks and lunch boxes bumping along the concrete, attached to tired little arms and little people who were already in tears about needing a snack (and a nap). The dads inevitably would scoop up the entire unit—kid, backpack, lunch box, whine—and haul it all to a waiting car.

And the cars. That's where I really needed my lawn chair.

There was a war raging in the parking lot. On one side were the people who appeared to have very few responsibilities in life and who showed up five hours before the final bell to sit in their cars. There they sat for hours, or maybe they never left after the first bell at 8:30 a.m. They staked out their position in the front of the line and They. Did. Not. Move. I swear I had seen some of them sit even after their children had entered the car, kind of like a subtle hand gesture to all the renegades who thought they could swoop in one minute before the bell rang and expect to find a spot in line.

This stubborn immobility drove the other parents bonkers. I'd seen glares, near sideswipes, snarls. I'd heard some language that the Character Counts section of the Springdale Elementary handbook would designate as "disrespectful." I'd seen one woman cry, like the mascara-running-down kind of cry typically reserved for the end of *Steel Magnolias*.

Nora and I would stick to our maple tree, thanks.

The bell rang and Nora came skipping out the front door, the ribbons from a curious looking art project trailing behind her. She was already headed toward our rendezvous point but I waved big anyway. My heart leaped a bit as she made her way through the crowd. Good grief, did I love that child.

"Hi, Mom," she said when she approached. I crouched down to hug her but she stiff-armed me. "Not so fast," she said. "You'll crush the mitochondria."

I stepped back to admire the art she displayed. She kept one arm outstretched to keep away the reckless huggers among us. "Wow," I said, taking in a tangled mess of ribbon and squiggles. Mitochondria bore a striking resemblance to Jelly Belly beans. "I'm afraid I'm not up on my mitochondria. Remind me what I learned in tenth grade biology. And also remind me why you're talking about mitochondria in kindergarten." I didn't know whether to feel smug about the use of my tax dollars or worried that Calypso was forgetting to teach things like the alphabet.

"Silly." Nora looked disappointed to have such a dolt for a mother. "Everyone knows that mitochondria help our bodies figure out how to breathe and how to have energy. And kindergartners have lots and lots of energy." Nora had taken to mimicking her teacher in a singsong voice. The first week it was endearing. Now it was testing my Christian forbearance.

"Thanks for the reminder, kiddo," I said, ready to steer the conversation away from the cellular level. If she started talking about organic chemistry, I was toast. "How was the rest of your day? Tell me about a time when you felt happy."

"Hmmm." Nora shrugged her ladybug backpack off her tiny shoulders and I transferred it to my own. She took my hand as we crossed the front lawn. We both startled when a car honked near us. I clutched my heart and Nora's hand more tightly but quickly realized the honker wasn't even looking at us but was attempting to tell another driver to move out of the middle of the three pickup lanes. I inferred by the look on her face that if that driver did not move out of the middle lane, the honker would need to get out of her car and start eating the wrongdoer's children. I hurried Nora away from the congestion and across the street. I relaxed when we stepped up the curb and onto the tree-lined sidewalk that led to our house.

"I felt happy," Nora said, "when Damian picked me to help him pass out his birthday treats. He brought vanilla wafers, which are delicious." She jumped over a crack in the sidewalk. "Damian is a little naughty. Sometimes he does a booty dance on the playground, which is inappropriate." Kindergarten was a lot of things, but to Nora, it was mostly a place where she could report on all things inappropriate. "But he's usually a good boy. And he hasn't pulled any cards. Not like Gus Hill."

"How did Gus Hill do today?" I'd found it was best to just ask this question straight up. No sense in putting it off because Nora had an OCD compulsion to give the Gus Hill status every evening. It was a lot like the weather report on the ten o'clock news. Not a lot of change, not a lot of interest, but we still got the full analysis, even if the Middle East had imploded and the president had fallen down six flights of stairs, naked, during a press conference. The naked president would have to wait until we knew how Gus Hill had fared.

"Two cards, one time-out, one missed recess." Nora shook her head. "I worry about that kid."

I bit back a smile. "What about a time when you felt sad?"

Nora stopped to pick up a bright yellow leaf that had fallen, one of the first of the season and striking in its beauty against the lush green that surrounded it. "Lila P. brought in a picture of her new baby sister. The baby's name is Sasha. I like that name, don't you?"

I nodded. "I do like that name. That's exciting for Lila and her family. What did the baby look like?" Despite the gnaw in my gut, I pressed on in this conversation, waiting for Nora to finish the bit about the baby so we could get back to her day. Not everyone in our house had to feel miserable every time a baby was brought up, right?

"She was really cute," Nora said. "Her face was pink and smooshed and she had a little bow in her hair. I don't know how that bow was stuck in there because Sasha doesn't really even have any hair. Maybe they used Gorilla Glue."

I laughed. "I hope not. Unless she wants to wear that bow for the rest of her life."

Nora giggled and I tried again. "So when did you feel sad today, Peanut?"

Nora furrowed her brow at me. "I just told you. When Lila P. showed me the picture of her baby sister."

My heart drooped. "Why did that make you sad, Norie?"

She hopped on one foot. "Because I want to have my own baby sister. And we keep missing all our babies."

My throat closed, the grief rising up and pulling it tight. *Missing our babies.* We had tried to be as honest as we could with Nora about why Jake and I were so sad sometimes, why some days I wanted to sit on the couch and cry for just a bit, why I had to go to the hospital for a long time and then came home groggy and red-eyed. Our versions of the story were sanitized, five-year-old-appropriate versions. We didn't want to frighten Nora, but we did want her to feel included in all of what life was, even the hard parts of life. We wanted her to know that we wanted a sibling for her desperately but that things weren't going quickly or easily. At some point, we must have used the verb *to lose*, that we had lost a baby. Losing and missing were very similar in Nora's book. And truth be told, her term was more accurate. We did keep missing our babies.

"I'm sorry you felt sad," I said finally.

Nora said nothing but she had stopped skipping. I tried to think of something wise to say, some way to neatly package her sadness and make sense of why we found ourselves stuck in this same spot, so many months into this gig. But before I could put together any words that didn't sound like they'd been on deep discount in the Hallmark store, Nora interrupted my thoughts.

"We should pray about this!" She sounded like she'd just discovered cotton candy in her backpack.

I demurred by murmuring a noncommittal assent.

"Right now," she said firmly. "We should pray about babies right now."

I looked around nervously, feeling suddenly exposed. Our street was totally empty save a group of fat squirrels running across the Havershams' perfect lawn. "I *have* prayed about it." I heard defensiveness creeping into my voice. "I've prayed about it a lot."

"We have to pray again." Nora had the look on her face that she got when I suggested maybe I should tie her shoes for her because we were running late. "The widow in the Jesus story banged on that judge's door a million times. Finally that sleepy judge got out of bed and helped her. Pastor Carter said we are supposed to not ever give up praying, even if it takes forever.

God always listens and He's not even sleepy. That part was just to help us have a picture in our minds."

Dang Pastor Carter and dang Sunday school and dang my daughter interpreting the Bible for me. God and I were at a bit of a rough spot lately, and I wasn't exactly seeking out extra time with Him. I looked at my daughter, starting to formulate a way in which to let her know that sometimes prayer was tricky. Sometimes God didn't answer the way we wanted, and it became painful to keep asking.

She pointed at me. "You pray first." She stopped in the middle of the sidewalk and closed her eyes. She still clutched the single perfect, yellow leaf in her hand. When I didn't say anything she cleared her throat, a new trick that she liked to employ when things weren't running at her preferred tempo. She said a word when she did it, something that sounded like, "Har-harm." Eyes still closed, "har-harm"-ing.

I rolled my eyes, partly at her and partly at God. Fine. "God, we thank you for this beautiful day and for Nora's school. Thank you that we can learn new things. Thank you that in our country, girls can get an education and are encouraged to do well. We know this isn't the case in many countries in the world."

Nora nudged me with her toe. "Ask for a baby."

Wow. The girl could sniff out a diversionary tactic from a hundred paces.

I sighed. "You know my heart and You know how many times I've asked but I'm asking again. Please allow me to have a baby. We'd love to have another child in our family." That's as far as I got. Tears filled my eyes. I dug my fingernails into my palms to stop them from escaping down my cheeks. "Your turn," I whispered to Nora.

"Dear Jesus," she said. "I would like a sister or brother,

please. I think we would be a very good family for a little baby. Please give us one so we can love it and take care of it and kiss it. And please give it smooshy cheeks. Amen."

Nora opened her eyes and looked satisfied. "There. We can do it again at bedtime." The woman was a German chancellor in the making. "Can I have pretzels and cheese for my snack?"

"Sure," I said. I was already falling behind as she ran ahead to our house. I watched her get after it, pumping her arms, legs all muscle, flying up the hill to our front walk. For the thousandth time, I marveled at how fast she was growing, muscles, bones, mind, heart. I took a deep breath and followed her, but I worried I would never catch up.

8

That evening, Jake came to find me as I was getting high. The finding was intentional; the getting high was not. After I'd finished the kitchen cabinet project, I'd spent a few aimless mornings wandering around the house while Nora was at school. My mind was restless but I knew how to fix that. I needed to paint all the furniture in my house.

Okay, not all. Just most.

I'd tackled Nora's dresser and two of our bedside tables and was now onto an old coffee table that may or my not have been buried under boxes in the attic before I resurrected it to give it another shot at coffee table-ing. Everyone deserved a second chance at being useful to society, I figured. Even yellowing oak with a 1970s silhouette.

Jake walked into the garage and choked on the fumes. "Geez, Heidi," he said, already opening a window. "You're going to asphyxiate. This is our lowest emission latex but you still need to ventilate." He plugged in a box fan sitting by the outlet. "I keep bringing this fan to wherever you're working and you keep not turning it on."

I shrugged, kept moving my paintbrush up one leg of the table in careful, methodical strokes. "Sorry. I don't really notice the fumes."

"That's because you're high," Jake said, his voice rising in pitch and volume. "I did not marry an addict. You have such nice teeth and hair. Why would you go down that road?"

I made a face at him. "I'm painting a coffee table. I don't even know how to mix up a batch of meth. I think we're safe."

Jake shook his head, mumbling something about a slippery slope.

"What do you think?" I gestured to the table. I'd finished priming and was starting on a first coat of color. "I think the gray is going to look so good. It's such a warm color for gray. It reminds me of cashmere."

Jake stared at the table for a beat, his face entirely blank. This was the same expression he employed after I came home from a particularly rough haircutting experience. I have a lot of unruly curls, so this had happened with regular frequency in our marriage. Finally he spoke. "Heidi, I love you. But that is one ugly table. So ugly, in fact, that no amount of *Vintage Pewter* in eggshell will change its fate. It's Ugly Table for the rest of its life."

I scowled at him, scowled at the table. "I think it's getting better. Way better."

"Where will you put this table, may I ask? After it's been *Vintage Pewter*ed?"

"Well," I said slowly, "I haven't really decided that yet. I'm sure I'll find a spot."

"That table is enormous," Jake said, starting to sound testy. "We don't have the space for it."

I turned to him, narrowing my eyes. "What's your deal? Did you honestly come out here to pick a fight about the coffee table?"

"No." The word was clipped. "Maybe. I just don't understand why you're spending so much time on this stuff."

I dipped my brush in the bucket and turned back to the table. "I like it. I like starting a project and then finishing it and having something to show for it. Plus, I get the paint for free so it only costs me my time."

"It's not free," Jake mumbled. "Nothing's free."

I let that hang. Jake knew that a quart of *Vintage Pewter* that someone else had mixed, paid for, and then returned in a huff because she meant to buy *Barndoor Grey was*, actually, free. But he seemed to be in a snit. I wasn't going to indulge him.

I painted in silence for a few minutes. The whir of the fan drowned out the movement of my brush across the table surface, but I knew it was there, quiet, steady, sure. I'd almost forgotten Jake was still leaning against the tool bench when he cleared his throat.

"So did you get a chance to look at the adoption stuff I printed out for you?"

I stiffened. When I glanced at him, he had crossed his arms. His jaw was set and his eyes bright. I suspected he already knew the answer to that question.

"Not quite yet." I tried to sound nonchalant as I started in on another leg on the table. "I've been so busy during the day, which is crazy. Before Nora went to school, I had visions of doing all these fantastic things with my newfound time." I was starting to babble, but I didn't even try to rein it in. "I wanted to start baking bread because I've always wanted to learn how to do that. And I wanted to clean all of our closets and the dungeon." This was our quasi-affectionate term for our basement. A basement in a hundred-year-old house does bring to mind certain scenes in *Silence of the Lambs*. "And I wanted to read and read and read. I have a list to beat all lists. But I have yet to start even one book." I shook my head, hoping my answer was convincing enough to let this cup pass from me. Just for tonight. I would think about it all tomorrow.

Jake didn't move. I felt him watching my face as I painted. Finally, he spoke, quietly. "I don't want to do this if you don't want to do this."

I looked at him. "Of course I do. I want a baby with everything I have." I paused the brush above the table, midair.

He sighed. "I just want you to look at the paperwork. Or watch some of the videos with me. Or read some of the FAQs on the hundreds of websites I've visited."

"Sorry," I said, not sounding one bit sorry but every bit hacked off. "I'm doing the best I can right now."

"Well, then, if this is your best, we need to stop the process." Jake threw his hands in the air. "You're not ready, Heids. Let's just admit that and move on."

"I'm *trying* to move on," I said through gritted teeth. My eyes stung. "This is what moving on looks like for me. Painting useless furniture and praying with Nora on the sidewalk and reading the paperwork you give me. But I have to do it my own way and in my own time. You can't bully me into it."

Jake made a strangled sound in his throat. "Bully you? Are you serious? You cannot be serious." He ran his hands through his hair. "We already talked about this. You said you were ready."

"I was." I blew out a sigh, my shoulders sagging. I felt like a punctured balloon. "I am. I'll read the adoption stuff tomorrow. I promise." I went back to my painting. I could feel my heart racing but I was dry-eyed. "Can we not talk about this anymore? I think we're dealing with this in different ways, Jake. And I just can't talk about it right now. I'll read it all tomorrow."

Jake said nothing for a long time. When he spoke, I could hear the effort he had to expend to get the words out. "I'm headed to bed. Don't forget to turn off the fan when you come in. You'll burn out the motor if it's on all night."

He walked away. I heard the door click shut and knew he was being careful not to slam it. Nora was sleeping and he didn't want to wake her. It was remarkable, the self-control one could summon when the price of losing it would cause a child to be cranky for the following twenty-four hours.

I watched my paintbrush coat the table and took care to cover every single imperfect spot. I took my time.

Jake was long asleep when I finally went to bed.

9

When I woke the next morning, I could not figure out why squirrels were in my room and why they were dancing the lambada. My eyelids were painfully heavy and it cost me to lift them. The squirrels were making all sorts of squirrel noises, chirping and running squirrel races around my head. And the music! Why was Jake not turning down the music? Was Jake dancing the lambada? I was already mad at the thought. I'd begged him to go to salsa night at El Calor for years and he would have none of it.

I propped myself up on one elbow, ready to give Jake a piece of my Latin dancing mind. Gradually our bedroom came into focus and I realized the squirrels were not actually running circles around our bed and on my face but were in fact running in the gutters outside my window. And the lambada was a chipper little tune vibrating from my phone alarm. I tugged the phone off my bedside table and squinted at the time.

My stomach dropped. The first bell was ringing along with the lambada. Nora was going to freak out.

I threw the covers off my body and ran out into the hallway. One should never endure childbirth and breastfeeding and then have to run into a hallway. The anatomy just didn't cooperate.

"Nora! Wake up, sweetie!" I called, skidding into her room. Bed made, shades up, no sign of the child. Good, I thought. She's up and probably munching Cheerios as I speak.

I took the stairs down two at a time, a risky endeavor considering I'd been with the hip-swiveling squirrels only moments before.

"Norie, honey!" I tried making my voice sound excited rather than panicked. I sounded like Julie Andrews on performance enhancing drugs. "Where are you, Nora? I overslept! We have to hurry!"

I found the note on the kitchen table.

Morning!

You didn't move when I tried to wake you, so I called in late and took Nora to school. Hope you're feeling okay. You were snoring. The last time you did that you had strep.

Are we still on for dinner with Willow and her online dude tonight?

Jake

I slumped into one of the kitchen chairs. Disaster avoided. Jake to the rescue. Nora was probably watching Gus Hill snort Wite-Out right that second. All was well.

My eyes drifted to the sheath of papers next to Jake's note. The paper on top had the logo for Hope's Reach and "Adoption FAQ" in large font. I picked it up and started to skim the facts, trying to register what 153 million orphans worldwide really looked like. I read about children escaping human trafficking and poverty, children abandoned when parents died, children needing homes and love and a mom and a dad. I saw photos of babies who had been placed in families, graphs showing what adoption looked like in the United States and abroad, testimonials from parents who pursued adoption after failed pregnancies, failed courses of IVF, never-ending waits for a child to fill the emptiness in their homes.

I closed my eyes and listened to my heart beating in my ears. I felt my thinking shift slightly, as if looking through a different cut of the same prism.

I did know that much, how to love a child. All children needed love, and Jake and I had a lot of that to offer.

Closer, I thought. I'm moving closer.

I sat at that table for a long time, watching the light as it slowly illuminated the room, lifting shadows and exposing the dark.

✦ ✦ ✦

Micah stood under the porch light and squeezed his eyes shut. "All right," he said. "I'm ready."

Nora took him by the hand and tugged.

"Step up!" I said hurriedly, relieved that Micah lifted one Converse high in the air to clear the last of the stairs. I smiled as he shuffled into the entryway of our house, unable still to absorb the adult Micah after knowing him for most of his tumultuous adolescence. I had taught Micah when he was in high school, and while he wasn't quite as disinterested in Spanish as the *cerveza* crowd, he was not exactly gunning for second language acquisition during those years. Piercings, yes. Rogue tattoos, yes. Bad poetry and slam dancing, absolutely. But verb conjugation, not so much.

And now Micah was finishing college with a business degree, thinking about MBA programs for the following year, and dating a girl that wore her natural hair color. I sighed, so proud, and resisted the urge to reach over and pinch his cheeks.

"Are we close?" he asked with exaggerated impatience. "I'm going to be an old, wrinkly man by the time we get there."

Nora giggled. "We aren't very close. So you might be getting wrinkles right this second."

Micah groaned, which educed another giggle from my daughter.

"Step!" I said again when he reached the bumpy spot where wood met kitchen tile. Micah pulled up one lanky leg again and stepped big.

"Three-two-one-blast-off go!" Nora cried and pulled on Micah's arm. He dropped his hand from his face and searched the counter until he saw Nora's surprise. "Jell-O alphabet letters! My very favorite things in the entire universe!" Then, dropping his voice, he added to me, "That is, other than the *mojitos* at El Calor. Smoothest rum ever."

I *tsk*ed. "You just keep your twenty-one-year-old self and your smooth rum away from my daughter or you're fired. I don't care if you've been her favorite babysitter since birth."

Micah looked injured. "I would never," he said, a little fiercely. And I grinned, letting him know that I knew. He might still have the rogue tats, and he might talk big about *mojitos*, but Micah was truly a total pushover for and utterly devoted to our daughter.

Jake walked into the room. He was a handsome man, my husband. I watched as he greeted Micah, asked him about his favorite classes this semester, talked shop with him regarding the current state of the S & P. I wanted to lean into him and put my head on his shoulder. I wanted to hug him right there and breathe in what I knew would be a delicious mixture of clean skin, cologne, and toothpaste. I wanted to blurt that I was trying, that I wanted to feel exactly what he felt about adoption and that

I was ready for everything to go back to normal between us. That this politeness that had descended was worse than an argument and that he should stop being so exasperatingly nice.

He turned to me then and I worked up a quick smile. I was becoming very adept with the quick-smile. I could quick-smile with the best of them. I turned my quick-smile on Micah, feeling like a TV meteorologist.

"All right then, you two crazy people."

Nora struck a disco pose and Micah mirrored her to the letter. She collapsed into giggles.

"Exactly," I said. I raised an eyebrow at Micah. "Dinner is pasta and sauce. I've grated some pecorino and there are trimmed snow peas to steam."

Micah made a face. "Geez, Mrs. Elliott. Just because I've given up ramen and learned a few things in the kitchen, that doesn't mean I'm ready to snow pea when I come over. What happened to the days of frozen pizza? Mac and cheese?"

"Yesyesyes!" Nora was jumping up and down. "Pizzapizzapizza!"

I frowned at them both. "You can ignore the peas but no pizza. I didn't buy any because I knew boiling water was now a part of your skill set."

Micah rolled his eyes.

"And you can call me Heidi, as you very well know. I feel like we have covered this ground before. Like once a month for the last three years." I gathered my purse from the kitchen table and Jake helped me slip into my coat.

"Never gonna happen," Micah said. He let Nora climb onto his back and they followed us to the front door. "Can't. You'll always be Mrs. Elliott to me. I like it that it makes you sound a little elderly." He grinned. Nora pretended to whip him like a horse to make him trot.

I shook my head. "If my daughter didn't think you were the kindergarten equivalent of hanging out with Sarah Jessica Parker and all her pals, I would have to let you go immediately for that kind of comment. No severance pay, either."

Micah started to trot. "Everything you just said is elderly in nature. I think Sarah Jessica Parker is about ninety years old at this point. *She* probably has a great severance package. And false teeth."

"Have fun, you two," Jake said. "We'll be home in a few hours."

Nora squealed, "Byeeeeee! Love you!"

I sniffed as we stepped onto the porch. "Whatever. Traitor."

Jake walked ahead to open my car door. "You look great," he said and leaned in to kiss me. I would use the descriptors *sanitized* and *gentlemanly* to describe that kiss. The passion police had no worries at the Elliott house in that moment. They could just pass on by, head over to the Havershams and hope for something a little more scandalous there. Mr. Haversham had the habit of patting Mrs. H. on the rear, so that would have done the trick.

"Thank you," I said, ready with the quick-smile. I tucked into the front seat and as he walked around to the driver's side, I closed my eyes. No one told a girl this on her wedding day, but marriage could really suck all the romance out of a perfectly promising evening.

10

Willow looked glowy. Was glowy a word? It was for Willow that night. Jake spotted her at a corner table by the window at Guido's and he put his hand on the small of my back to guide me there. I couldn't see the online dude, but that was probably fine because I couldn't take my eyes off Willow. Her face was radiant. Her eyes shone, even from half a restaurant a way. She wore a black dress I hadn't seen before and I noticed more of a plunge in the neckline than was her typical style, though considering her history with bralessness, a little plunge to her probably felt like a Laura Bush imitation.

We approached the table and Willow looked up. She clasped her hands and her smile widened.

"You're here!" she said and rose to hug me. "You look lovely," she said, gesturing to my emerald green dress. "Wear more green. It brings out ocean blue in your eyes." She hugged Jake and he kissed her on the cheek. Turning to the man on her left, she said, "Heidi and Jake Elliott, this is Beau Vaughn. Beau, meet two of the best." Willow looked so happy, I could barely divert my gaze to main attraction.

"It's wonderful to finally meet you." Beau reached out to shake my hand, then Jake's.

We all agreed about how wonderful it was before taking seats at the cozy four-top. Jake asked Beau about his trip to Minneapolis and I peeked over my menu to get a good look. There was no way to get around it: Beau was fifty-year-old eye candy. The dude could have been on a toothpaste commercial. Or a Viagra one, but I tried not dwell on that. He had a full head of thick dark silvery hair and his slightly receding hairline only made him look more distinguished. Bright and curious brown eyes were framed by tanned wrinkles that deepened when he smiled, which was often. His teeth were a marvel, likely veneers and likely representing thousands of dollars. Annie would have been impressed. I was taking in his smartly tailored suit and wondering what he did to have defined pecs at an age when AARP came a-calling, when he turned to me and I had to pretend I was listening.

"Heidi, Willow tells me you used to teach Spanish at the high school."

I nodded. "I did. It feels like a million years ago, but at one time I was paid for all the hours I worked in a day." Too snarky? I thought. Too discontent? Too much of the culture wars too soon? I glanced at Willow, hoping for a nonverbal thumbs up, but she was staring at Beau, waiting for his response.

He spoke in perfect Spanish. "I'm sure you were an excellent teacher. What a loss for your students that you decided to stay home with your daughter."

I stumbled into a response, also in Spanish. "Thank you. I do miss teaching. But I know I made the right decision for our family." I switched to English. "You speak beautiful Spanish. Where did you learn?"

He shrugged. "A little here, a little there. I used to travel a lot for work. And we had a nanny while the kids were growing up.

She taught me a lot."

I narrowed my eyes, picturing a young, nubile Latin beauty, poolside, throwing her head back as she laughed with Beau and his children.

"María Elena was tough as nails," Beau continued. "She was old enough to be my mother and she didn't let me forget it when she would correct my pronunciation."

Willow laughed easily and I sat back a bit in my chair. All right, so the nanny wasn't nubile. And his pronunciation had been beaten out of him. I took a sip of water and tried to relax.

A server approached with a bottle of wine and turned the label for Beau's approval. He nodded and opened his hand toward Willow. "The lady should have the honor."

Willow looked a little like she'd just been crowned Queen of Everything. She took a cautious sip of the merlot and nodded her assent. I tried catching her eye again, knowing she hated red wine and would have preferred a cold hard cider any day of the week, but she was convincing as she said, "It's perfect. Thank you."

"I hope you don't mind that I took the liberty of ordering a few appetizers." Beau nodded to the servers who were approaching our table through a sea of flickering candlelight. "I know the chef and he likes to show off his best work. So I figured I'd let him."

"Sounds great to me," Jake said, already tucking into a platter of roasted tomatoes, ribbons of prosciutto, and burrata cheese, flecks of fresh basil dotting the plate. "I hope you order my entrée too. Less stress for a guy who knows best how to order a steak and fries."

"Me, too, please," Willow said with a soft laugh. "I like a chef who can show off."

Beau looked to me for my response and I let my quick-smile get some play around a hurried bite of burrata. I nodded, hoping that was sufficient to indicate my own assent. Sure. Order our food. Order for three of the most opinionated eaters I'd ever known. I kept that quick-smile in place, playing along for Willow's sake. We could talk later about how our brains had momentarily malfunctioned in the glow of candlelight and Beau's charm, when the merlot had mellowed and we'd returned to our senses. It would even be fun, I thought, to giggle about how we'd gotten caught up in the moment.

I tried a bite of the grilled green beans and garlic and let out an involuntary moan of appreciation. "Good grief. That lemon finish is brilliant," I said.

Beau nodded. "I agree. The citrus cuts through the earthiness of the beans and garlic. Very smart of Paulo. I'll tell him we said so." Beau winked at me before taking another bite.

"How is it that you know Paulo?" I said, saying the chef's name as if I was about to add "if that is his real name." I swallowed, trying to sound less like the prosecution. "Did you grow up together in Minneapolis?"

I saw the slightest flicker of—anxiety? irritation?—pass through Beau's gaze but it was gone as soon as it registered. "No, nothing like that. I've simply brought many clients here over the years. We've struck up a friendship, mostly defined by me spending thousands of dollars at his restaurant and complimenting him on his food."

He and Willow laughed. Jake nodded appreciatively but the appreciation seemed mostly reserved for the house-made focaccia he was devouring.

"I see," I said, not quite finished with my questions. I persisted, trying to graft them seamlessly into the rest of the meal, trying not to alert Willow that I was digging for something that lurked underneath the perfectly pressed shirt and suit that had likely cost three months' worth of a teacher's salary.

Here, in order of course consumed, is what I learned:

*Warm salad involving fried Brussels sprouts and pancetta: Beau grew up in Minneapolis and lived there all of his life, leaving only for college and for a brief stint to try out small-town life in a rural suburb of the Twin Cities.

*Pasta course of house-made sweet potato ravioli filled with braised beef and topped with sage and some kind of nectar of the gods: Nothing. I gleaned nothing during this course. I couldn't concentrate on anything but the nectar.

*Monkfish with prosciutto and artichokes: First, I learned that Jake had never heard of monkfish. The four of us spent a considerable amount of time discussing why, in fact, the fish that tasted so indulgent could be named after men who didn't, ahem, major in the sensual. But that could have been the prosciutto talking. Second, I learned that Beau, not a monk, had been married once and had two adult children. The divorce, he said, was difficult but amicable. No grandchildren.

*Chocolate and pistachio biscotti with espresso: This is where I learned I have no self-control. I was not one bit hungry, not even close. I was the exact opposite of hungry. But those biscotti (and I do mean the plural) found their way to me and I was so happy to guide them there. I also learned that Beau was very smooth in picking up the check. Jake was typically quite adept at forcing his hand but he didn't stand a chance with Beau. The bill was paid before the rest of us had even blotted the final chocolate crumbs off our faces.

A man in chef's whites approached our table as we were finishing our espressos. Beau stood to greet him in a slappy man-embrace and then turned to the three of us.

"Chef Paulo Moretti, the architect of what we just ate."

We clapped for Paulo. Paulo deserved applause.

He bowed slightly, and I judged from his girth that he was the taste tester. "Thank you for coming to dine with us this evening. I'm so pleased to hear you enjoyed your meal." He cuffed Beau on the shoulder. "This man is a good man, no? I have known him for many years. And have seen many beautiful women on his arm, but none so beautiful as you, madam."

Willow accepted the compliment with grace, but I narrowed my eyes at Beau. What kind of women? Was he dating all these women? Did the "clients" he'd cited need to be "on his arm" in order to get their biscotti? My internal air quotes were going haywire.

Chef Paulo took leave of us after a few more back slaps and compliment trading, and we soon threaded our way through the dining room and outside to the crisp autumn air.

"What do you think?" Willow whispered into my ear as we hugged good-bye.

We held onto the hug so we could chat. "He's very generous. And extremely handsome."

"I know," Willow said excitedly. "He really, really is." She pulled back from our embrace, still holding onto my arms. "I'm so happy you met him and that you like him. I knew you would." Her face was lit from within. I had never had the joy of meeting Michael, but I wondered if this was how she looked when she had spent an evening with him.

I squeezed Willow's arms and pulled out the quick-smile, which deserved some sort of commission for all the work it was getting that evening. "You kids have a good night. We're off to rescue our babysitter."

Beau shook my hand as we parted. "It was a true pleasure to meet you and Jake, Heidi," he said. His eyes fixed on mine. "I'm finding Willow has excellent taste in most things, and her choice of friends is no exception."

"Thank you for dinner," I said. "If you ever need us to help you compliment Chef Paulo again, we are willing participants."

Beau's laugh was easy. "Duly noted. I'm sure we'll be seeing lots of each other from here on out."

Willow looked so happy, I thought she might start tap-dancing. She'd done this once for Nora's benefit, and considering the flailing and huffing and puffing, I took Jake's hand and started for our car in order to spare her (and us).

I was still waving at the happy couple when I started in.

"Oh. My. Gosh," I said. "This is horrible. What are we going to do?"

"Huh?" Jake said. He screwed up his face in confusion. "Do about what?"

I shook my head. "There is something very off about that guy." I let out a pent-up sigh. "Willow can't date him. He's not right for her at all."

"I thought he was great." Jake shrugged. "The ultra-bleached teeth were a little jarring at first but I got used to it. And the guy can order food, I'll give him that. I hope he asks us to dinner again. Like tomorrow."

I rolled my eyes. "Don't get distracted by the prosciutto, Jake!"

"Okay, fine, but what about the fried Brussels sprouts? Or that sweet potato ravioli stuff? Genius."

"No," I said firmly. "There is something definitely sketch about this guy."

"The biscotti? You cannot deny that the biscotti was off the hook."

I ignored him, though I could still taste the chocolate and was considering Dumpster diving at the end of Paulo's shift. "He's too good to be true," I insisted. "Who has an amicable divorce these days?"

"Um," Jake said, "Gwyneth Paltrow? Lots of amicable there. The uncoupling was a wild success."

"But real people," I said. "What real people have amicable divorces? He can't be serious."

Jake turned onto our street. "Lots of people have them. What good were all those years of Oprah and Dr. Phil if we can't divorce amicably in this country?"

"And what about the many, many beautiful women on his arm through the years?" I'd slipped into my best Italian accent to conjure up Paulo's voice. I thought I nailed it but Jake didn't seem to notice. "Who were these women? And what was his yearly average? Two a year? Fifteen a year? Fifty-two each calendar year?" My voice was getting a little shrieky.

"Heids," Jake said as we pulled into the garage. "I think you're overthinking this. Willow found a great guy to date. They're just dating. Don't freak out yet."

I nudged my car door shut and followed him to the back door like a caffeinated Yorkie following a Great Dane. Chocolate biscotti *and* espresso, people. "I have to freak out *now*. Now is the perfect time to freak out. If I wait to freak out, I will miss the freak-out window!"

Jake removed his hand from the doorknob and turned to me. He had a slow smile forming on his lips, but his eyes looked tired. His shoulders slumped as he leaned against the door. Speaking quietly so Micah wouldn't hear, he said, "I love you. You're crazy in the head, and I love you." His kiss was tender, maybe a little cautious. "Stop freaking out. He's fine. We're all fine," he added, though now it looked like he was the one that needed convincing.

I stood on the garage step for an extra moment before going into the house, still hearing the echo of Jake's words.

11

Nora and I were having trouble with our efficiency and we could blame no one but ourselves. The conditions for leaf raking were ideal: sun blocked only occasionally by marshmallow clouds, not too cold, no wind. The issue was motivation. As in, we didn't have much.

"Okay," I said again. "After this jump, we are going to put this pile into bags."

"Yeehaw!" Nora said by way of response. She cartwheeled arms and legs into the mountain of red, orange, yellow, and the intermittent green. When she sat up, she had leaves stuck in her hair and on her clothes. A red leaf the size of a dinner plate clung to her cheek. She thrust two fists into the air. "I am the champion."

"Champion of what?" I asked, tugging a mostly empty yard waste bag over to the pile.

"Champion of jumping into big piles of leaves," Nora said in the Calypso Charm singsong. That voice was enough to make a person start questioning her own IQ score. "Don't have that snotty look on your face, Mom," Nora said still in singsong. "In Room 12 we celebrate each other's accomplishments."

"Ah," I said, as if the light bulb had just sputtered itself on.

"Good to know. I apologize for my snotty look." It took great effort not to roll my eyes as I said those words, but I did it. Parenthood was nothing if not a grand exercise in willpower. "Hey, Room 12 champ, will you please hold this for me?" I nudged the bag with my toe and held a full rake's worth of leaves over the opening at the top.

"Of course," Nora said. She skipped over, which was a remarkable cardio endeavor considering the ocean of leaves she had to plow through to get to me. Jake and I were also champions, only our title was Last People To Rake. We handily took down the competition every year as we lived on a street inhabited almost entirely by retirees. Nora and I were getting a start on the raking today so that Jake wouldn't have as much to do. Jake tended to mutter obscenities about people who had no jobs while he was raking, and considering we lived with a parrot who would likely repeat such statements not only to our jobless neighbors but also to the fine folks of Room 12, I thought it my civic duty to get a jump on the project.

"Mommy, when are you coming to help in Room 12 again?" Nora held the bag as long as no leaves were falling from my rake. At that point, she dropped the bag and tried catching the leaves. We were getting nowhere.

"Well," I said slowly, "Ms. Charm and I decided it might be better for me to help her with getting supplies ready for you and your classmates. Like making sure she has enough copies of a paper, stapling things, filing things. Stuff like that."

Nora nodded. She had stopped trying to catch leaves and wore a somber expression. "Gus Hill is still wearing his Band-Aid, even though it's black and fuzzy."

I might have thrown up a little in my mouth.

"He pulled a card today," she went on. "Ms. Charm said he

wasn't allowed to lick people but he did anyway."

I must have shown on my face the horror I felt.

"Don't worry," Nora said, waving away my fears with a shake of her head. "He didn't lick me. I told him if he did my dad would come over to his house and beat him up."

I bit my bottom lip, trying not to smile. Jake the Avenger. He'd threatened as much over the years, mostly in jest, though an illicit lick might very well have pushed him to action. Poor Gus Hill. Before the end of the year, he might have both Elliott parents gunning for him.

"Hey," I said with an enthusiasm I hoped was Room 12 appropriate. "I heard some big news about kindergarten. Ms. Charm wrote in her newsletter yesterday that at the end of the month, you get to wear your Halloween costume to school and march in the halls."

"The Parade of Wonder!" Nora squealed. She had now completely abandoned her post and was on the ground, flapping her arms and legs in an autumnal version of a snow angel. "Every other class calls it the Harvest Parade but Room 12 calls it the Parade of Wonder. Because we are *wonder*ful."

I leaned on my rake and stared at my daughter. "Does Ms. Charm require you to drink any particular Kool-Aid?"

Nora giggled. "No, silly. Our choices for lunch are water, white milk, and chocolate milk. I always, always, always have chocolate. It's the best and it makes me run faster at recess."

"Not fast enough to get away from your mom!" I threw down my rake and charged. She tried to crawl away but I caught her by the sneakers. We were giggling and getting all sorts of leaves everywhere but piles and bags when I caught movement at the corner of my eye. Nora noticed too. She twisted out of my hold and looked at the car pulling into the driveway.

"Annie!" Nora squealed. She wiggled out of my grasp and scrambled to her feet. Annie barely made it out of the driver's seat before getting tackled.

"Hey, kiddo," she said, folding over Nora to hug her. Annie's shoulder muscles flexed as she hugged my daughter and I tried remembering I was a Christian and that Christians weren't supposed to covet. Hair in a high ponytail and wearing three shades of Spandex, it looked like Annie was getting ready to go running. Annie ran, as in marathons and half marathons and 5K "fun runs." I had all sorts of reservations on the fun quotient of running, namely that it didn't exist. Annie knew my reservations after her many failed attempts to get me to go with her. Inevitably after the first half mile, I started whining and wondering why she hated me and what part of her childhood, unknown to me until that point, had forced her to become a sadist.

She didn't ask much anymore.

"How's the fancy kindergartner?" She stepped back to evaluate Nora. "You look mature. And smarter. Kind of like a short librarian."

Nora laughed. "I'm not short! I'm the fourth tallest girl in my class."

"My mistake," Annie said, laughing. "You're a tree."

Nora stood on her tiptoes, trying to look as treelike possible.

"Hey, lady," I said from across the yard. "Come over here and talk to me while I work. My assistant has proved to be very entertaining but a total bum when it comes to productivity."

Annie crossed to me in a few long-and-lean strides. Again with the Tenth Commandment. She put her hands on her hips and looked to be evaluating my progress. "Right," she said. "I see a few abandoned piles and lots of indentations roughly the size of Nora. When I pulled up, I believe you two were wrestling."

She smiled, and I thought I saw nostalgia in her eyes. "Take it from the productivity obsessed. The wrestling is a better choice."

"Going for a run?" I said, starting to rake again. One of the many perks of having a friendship as old and deep as the one I had with Annie was that yard work while conversing was completely socially appropriate, as was tooth brushing, talking with one's mouth full, and going to the bathroom. True story. This was real friendship.

"Yes," Annie said. She picked up a leaf to twirl between her fingers. "James is meeting me at the river path." She shifted on her feet. "He wanted to stop by too but I told him I'd meet him there."

I paused, crouched over a new pile. I looked at Annie. Her voice had changed suddenly and she looked exactly how she did in high school speech class right before it was her turn. "Annie?" I dropped my rake and walked toward her. "Is everything all right? Is it James? Is everything okay between you two?"

Tears were already spilling down her cheeks. She brushed them away with impatient strokes. "No. I mean, yes. James is fine. He's great. Things with him are great. *Really* great."

I chuckled, knowing they were still newlyweds and hearing all the "really" in that "*really* great."

"Okay, good," I said gently. "But you're crying."

Annie nodded. She searched my eyes before blurting it out. "Heids, I'm pregnant."

I took in a sharp breath and held it. A shot of adrenaline made my fingers tingle and I suppressed a sudden, violent urge to sob. I pulled Annie to myself, more an act of self-preservation than of congratulations. I needed time to compose my face.

"Annie, that's fantastic," I said as we hugged. My eyes burned. I blinked furiously. "I'm so, so happy for you." Sometimes we spoke what we wanted, not what we already possessed.

Annie clung to me. I could feel her body trembling. "I'm so sorry, Heidi."

I pulled back and made her face me.

"No." I shook my head. "Do not be sorry. This is phenomenal, beautiful news. Please don't be sorry for me. I'm really, really happy." By now tears were falling freely down *my* face. We looked at each other, both crying and looking miserable and insisting we were happy.

Nora had stopped carving a long line of cartwheels along the perimeter of the yard. She stopped a few feet away from us and looked at me, looked at Annie. "Why is everybody crying? Is it PBJ?" Her lip quivered at the memory of our hamster, three years dead but whose memory still evoked a torrent of emotion for some of us.

Annie nodded at me, tears starting anew, and I knew she wouldn't be able to say it again. So I said it for her.

"Norie, guess what?" I gathered her into our little circle. "Annie has a surprise. The best kind of surprise. She's going to have a baby."

Nora's eyes widened, first at me and the words coming out of my mouth, then at Annie's face, then down to her infuriatingly flat belly.

"A baby?" she said quietly.

Annie nodded. Her smile was shaky and her face was starting to blotch. "A baby, kiddo. It won't be here for a long time, but it's in there." She put a hand protectively on her stomach. "It's growing and growing and someday it will be as big and tall as you. Maybe even fourth tallest in the class."

Nora kissed Annie's hand that rested on her abdomen. "Hi, baby. I'm Nora." Switch to Room 12 singsong: "I'm always going to be bigger than you, but don't worry. You can still play with some of my toys as long as you don't slobber all over them."

Annie laughed and grabbed Nora into a tight hug.

Nora looked at me over Annie's shoulder. "We're going to have a baby too. Right, Mom?"

I nodded, summoning just a bit of the courage and faith my daughter continued to have in this agonizing process.

"We are," Nora insisted, still wrapped in Annie's arms. "We are asking God every day and pretty soon, He's going to tell us yes."

I closed my eyes, lifting my face in a sudden cool breeze, waiting for the ache to pass, waiting for God to break His silence, waiting, waiting.

12

Slipping underneath the striped awning and the bright and beautifully lettered sign reading "Elliott Paints," I took a moment to quiet my breathing before tugging on the front door. I was in silent sleuth mode and I was pretty much crushing it. I hadn't dressed in *Mission: Impossible* black or worn a ski mask or anything. I did have *some* self-respect. But I did use the left side door, the one that didn't have a bell to announce my entrance. Making a visual sweep of the store I saw Rob Jeffries, Jake's longtime cohort and most trusted employee. Rob had his back to me and was chatting with a customer by the tarps and tape. I stepped heel-to-toe and wished I were wearing moccasins, or at least not the squeaky rubber soles of my tennis shoes. I kept one eye on Rob, who did not appear to hear the squeak.

Reaching the small section of returned paints, I lowered quietly to sit on the spotless linoleum. I scanned the labels on the cans. *Terra-Cotta Steps*, no . . . *Mouse Gray*, ew . . . *Emotion?* *Emotion?* What the heck did that mean? Which emotion, for the love of Pete? Anger? Distaste? Unfettered joy? There was no thumb imprint of the color . . . maybe I could sneak a paint chip from the opposite side of the store. *Dead Salmon.* I stared at that one a good long while and surmised that this was not the first time that unfortunate name had found itself on the return shelf. I picked up the abandoned quart next to the salmon. Ooh, different, better death: *Death By Chocolate*. Oh, yes, please.

I had one hand on a pint of *Come Sail Away* and was wishing it were eggshell, not flat finish, when Rob cleared his throat. "You can squat but you cannot hide. Step away from the discounts."

I groaned and twisted around to look way, way up. Rob was six foot eleven, which was a very long way from where I sat. I frowned at him. "You're not the boss of me."

Rob raised an eyebrow from its position near the ceiling tiles. "You want to test that theory? Your husband has warned me that if I give you anything more from this section, I will need to look elsewhere for employment. As you know, four children and a sassy wife live at my house. I'm going to need to keep my job."

I stood and brushed imaginary dust off my rump. "Fine, fine. I can't have you begging on street corners and have myself to blame. Plus, panhandling is against city code, so then I'd have to come bail you out of jail and the guilt would just be too much."

Rob grinned. "Apart from your unstable mental state, how's it going?"

I shook my head. "Not instability. A gift. A talent, only recently discovered because my child flew the coop and I finally have the 'me-time' I griped about not having for the last five years."

Rob nodded. "You're going nuts."

"Pretty much."

"And I heard Nora has that Salsa or Cha-Cha woman for a teacher." He winced. "Janie had her. Total weirdo."

We started toward the back of the store and Jake's office. "Yes. Calypso Charm, which may or may not be her real name,"

I said.

"Don't worry. The damage will be minimal. Kids are resilient. Janie only cried herself to sleep for half of first grade."

I gasped and started to protest but Rob laughed. He slapped me on the back and I jumped. Sometimes Rob forgot we weren't all forwards on his college basketball team.

"Oops," he said, chagrined. "Samantha hates it when I do that. Old habits and all that."

I laughed. "No problem. Just don't try to chest bump me. That could get awkward, especially since my nose would be eye-level with your nipples."

At the mention of nipples, Jake looked up from the papers on his desk.

"You're talking about Rob's nipples." He said it as a statement, not a question.

"Yes," I said, face serious. "And I think it's about time. Have *you* ever asked Rob about his nipples? And how long have you two worked together?"

Rob shook his head. "Don't let her distract you, boss. I found this woman rummaging through the forbidden fruit. I thought you should know." Rob winked at me and gave me a fist bump. "Say hi to Nora for me. Tell her she'll graduate out of Cha-Cha's class and start learning how to count eventually."

I made a face as he loped away, chuckling at his own joke.

Jake stood from his desk and came to lean against it. He tugged my hand and pulled me to him. After a long, slow kiss, I pulled back, smiling.

"Wow. Is this how you treat all your shoplifters? Because that might not actually deter them from becoming repeat offenders."

He kissed me again. "Nope. Just the shoplifters I'm sleeping with."

I cocked me head, narrowed my eyes. "Um, that's not the most comforting response."

He chuckled and walked back to his desk chair. "You're the only shoplifter I'm sleeping with."

"Again with the lack of comfort."

He smiled at me and I felt my heart jump. Still swoon-worthy, after all these years.

"Nora get off to school okay?" he said.

I plopped down onto the chair opposite him. It was made of hardwood, so the plopping kind of hurt. "Yes. I helped her carry in her show-and-tell, which, as you might guess, is not called show-and-tell in Room 12. It's called share-and-remember."

Jake shuddered. "That lady is cuckoo for Cocoa Puffs. Are you sure we shouldn't try having Nora switched to a different section? Are we screwing up our daughter by letting her hang out with share-and-remember all day?"

I shook my head. "Nah. Nora's fine. Her handwriting is getting really good, she's learning one column addition, and she's already reading at a third grade level."

He sniffed. "She knew all of that before she stepped foot in Calypso Honeypot's classroom."

I giggled. "That woman's parents should be ashamed for the way they named her. It's fortunate she's turned to interpretive dance and rainbows and moonbeams. I might have become bitter and angry. Changed my name to something sensible and become an accountant."

He pointed toward the top sheet on a stack of papers. "Speaking of how we'd be awesome parents of two children, I was just reading about Hope's Reach."

"Were we just talking about how we'd be awesome parents of

two children?"

He grinned. "Not really. But sometimes you need me to remind you that we would. I'm really good at segues."

"Right." I smiled back. This was good. This was normal. Not weighted and fraught. Just normal. I took a deep breath and a half step forward. "What are you reading?"

Jake paused a second, and I could see he was surprised I hadn't shut down the conversation. As I said, a half step.

"Well," he said, excitement already creeping into his voice in that one word. "I was reading about how they encourage you to meet with their director. Lots of couples have questions, this says, and a meeting with the director might be a good place to have those questions answered." He ran his finger down the sheet until he reached the spot he was seeking. "Her name is Moira Kapoor."

I felt my brow furrowing. "Irish? Or Indian?"

Jake shrugged. "Probably both. And definitely better than Cha-Cha Honeypot. This woman must have had compassionate parents."

I took a deep breath and let it out slowly. "Okay. Let's meet with Moira." I stood before I lost my nerve. "This week. Let's meet this week."

Jake didn't even try to hide his glee. "Great! I'll call her this afternoon! This week! Great!"

"To ask questions," I said in my best hall monitor voice. "We still have a way to go."

"Right. Absolutely," said the father who once purchased an adult-sized potter's wheel after his four-year-old daughter formed a perfect pinch pot in the sandbox and had asked about clay. The man wasn't big on stop signs. He put one hand on his cell phone and I could see the effort it was taking not to call Moira

Kapoor right that second.

I stood and ignored the dread in my stomach. "See you tonight."

I waved to Rob as I opened the door to the outside. Clouds were blocking the sun and I shoved my hands into my pockets as I took to the sidewalk, making my way, one step at a time.

✦ ✦ ✦

An hour later, I emerged from LaSalle's Market, heavy laden with too many bags of groceries for a woman of my height. I made my way down one block of sidewalk, careful not to trip or to bump into anyone passing. I stumbled a bit on the uneven pavement in front of Gigi's Hair, and I muttered aloud about people fixing their sidewalks instead of worrying so much about their highlights. The full bags had started to feel like I'd been shopping at the nearest lead factory and my scalp tingled with sweat. My foul mood dipped further when I remembered Jake's call that came in while I was in the produce section. He'd practically yodeled about a meeting with Moira Kapoor that he'd scheduled for the day after next. A grown man should never yodel, I'd decided as I was stuffing Italian parsley into a plastic green sleeve. It was beneath him. Only an hour removed from when I'd given him the green light to schedule this meeting, I was nowhere near matching his Alpine enthusiasm. Judging from my reaction to a firm date for my baby step forward, I would have been wise to keep my mouth shut until I was fully ready to meet Ms. Kapoor.

I sighed now, remembering the sting of feeling at odds with Jake's joy. An uncharacteristically hot October sun beat down on my curls, which were enduring a particularly lackluster day. The curls were all frizz, no body, no softness, and I considered turning around to get a different shampoo at Gigi's but I was just getting to the point where the pain in my arms and hands was numbing. No need to open up all that blood flow and start over.

I was just one block away from where I'd parked and could feel the dent between my eyebrows deepen as I concentrated on the final push when I saw Willow approaching, her arm linked with Beau's. I saw them before they saw me. Willow was very animated, telling a story, and Beau face was relaxed and smiling. He was matching her pace, though his legs were much longer than hers.

I composed my face to appear as if the grocery sacks weren't making deep and life-threatening divots in my palms. "Hey, you two," I said as I stopped under an ash tree that spread a gold canopy of leaves over the sidewalk.

"Heidi!" Willow guided Beau over to me. Did I imagine it or did he look considerably less pleased than Willow to see me?

"Good grief, friend, set those bags down," Willow clucked. "They look horribly heavy."

"Here," Beau said. He reached for one of the bags. "Allow me."

"Oh, no," I said, holding tight to the bag even as he tried to pry it gently away. I saw either determination or arrogance in his expression and I didn't like either one. "I'm fine," I said. "Good for my biceps."

Willow looked at me, disbelieving. "Heidi, a gentleman is offering to carry your groceries. Why in the world would you deny him?"

"Wow," I said with a tight laugh. "When you make it sound so Jane Austen-ish . . ." I trailed off but still gripped my bags.

Beau appeared to be studying my face. Then he said, "Suit

yourself, but let me know if it gets to be too much."

"I will," I said in my best camp counselor voice. "Thanks for the offer. So what are you two kids up to?"

Willow looked at Beau, her face alight. "Oh, you know. Letting Sophie take the counter at the café for awhile so I can show off my hometown."

I shifted the bag with canned goods so it no longer gouged my hip. "This must seem absolutely sleepy next to Minneapolis," I said to Beau. "Are you itching for some traffic? Good ethnic food? The Guthrie?"

He laughed. "Well, I did have to control my rage when a guy took a fifteen full minutes to drive around the town square."

Willow leaned toward me and spoke in a conspiratorial voice. "Hank McCoy. Mabel was in the front seat."

"Ahh," I said, nodding. "You could have written a short master's thesis while you waited."

"Exactly," Beau said. "I started to worry about a medical issue but Willow assured me this was business as usual for the McCoys." He smiled at her as if her McCoy assessment would be Pulitzer material if she'd just submit it to the committee.

"You aren't a total newbie to the small town gig, though, right?" I said. Oh, how I wanted to dump those bags at the foot of the ash tree and just leave them there. I looked at Beau's arms and thought them to be more than capable, at least for my canned goods. I was close to asking when his words stopped me short.

"I'm afraid I am. Springdale is a whole different animal to me. Minneapolis has been home for so long." He was looking at Willow as he spoke and said the words as if they were coming from a place far away, someplace not as interesting as Willow's face.

I frowned. "I thought you said you'd lived in a small town during college."

"Pardon?" Beau said, but the snap of his head in my direction told me he'd heard me fine. "Oh. Right. College. That feels like such a long time ago, I'm afraid I sometimes feel it never happened."

My brow was fully furrowed. I was also inching up in years but I had yet to *forget college*. "And didn't you mention a time when you lived outside the Cities?" I tried to maintain a friendly tone but Beau's lack of concentration and the bags and my heat-seeking head of frizz—it was all beginning to beat me down.

Willow looked at Beau long enough that she nudged him. "Beau? Tell Heidi about Brookside."

"Right," Beau said, looking relieved. "Brookside. I lived there at one point, but I didn't last. I knew fairly early into the experiment that I would need a good cup of coffee and a carpool lane if I was going to feel at home in the world."

Willow scoffed. "You know my café serves a better cup of coffee than any Starbucks."

Beau cocked his head in thought. "Let me think about that before answering."

Willow elbowed him, hard enough that he yelped. "Think fast. And," she wagged her finger at him, "you don't need a carpool lane in Springdale. That's why we *live* in Springdale. To escape things like carpool lanes."

"Aha," Beau said, triumphant. "Not so, my dear. I think we learned this morning that Springdale is the perfect place for a carpool lane. Enter the McCoys."

I cleared my throat and spoke above the sound of their laughter. "Well, I'll leave you two to the tour. Willow, I'll call you later. Beau," I said, doing my best to keep my tone convincing, "great to see you again."

I felt Willow's gaze linger as I walked away. I was never very good at lying to her. Dumping all the bags roughly into my Civic, I stood a minute under the puny shade of the opened trunk, feeling the blood rush back into my upper limbs.

"What are you hiding?" I asked aloud. I peeked above the roofs of the cars parked alongside mine and saw Willow and Beau stopped outside the bookstore. Willow was pointing to a particular cover and Beau soon took her hand and held the door as she entered the store.

I slammed the trunk shut. I turned the key in the ignition and waited while all four windows slowly rolled down to let the heat escape. Setting my jaw, I started toward home.

Small town, maybe, but we did have the Internet. It was time for me to figure out what, exactly, was so very wrong about Beau Vaughn.

13

Groceries unpacked, I curled up to my laptop. On the coffee table in front of me was a plate with a pathetic looking turkey sandwich and a handful of Cheetos. I made a face at it as my computer powered on. One of these days, I thought, I'm going to start eating like an adult when I'm only feeding myself. Most nights of most weeks, I made balanced meals for our little family. Nora knew what couscous was, for example, and I'd perfected the medium-rare cut of beef for Jake. I felt I was fulfilling my role as a distant cousin or maybe just an admirer of Betty Crocker. But when it came time each day to make my own lunch, I regressed to my first year of college. I couldn't even blame this on Nora's new all-day kindergarten adventure. The ramen and mac-and-cheese and Cheetos started long before then.

I took my first bite and pulled up Google. An initial search of "Beau Vaughn" yielded a full screen of links and images. Beau with very attractive clients, nearly all of them women, and all of them associated with the name of his consulting firm. Beau cutting a ribbon at a new business. Beau representing the good people of the world on several nonprofit boards based in the Twin Cities. Beau shaking hands with the leader of the Republican Party of Minnesota.

I gasped at that one, not because I had any beef with Republicans but because Willow certainly did. She'd campaigned for Howard Dean even *after* he'd screeched, if that said anything. Over the years, I'd sat through more than a dozen diatribes during which she walked me through the rise of the women's movement, starting with Dolly Madison and bringing us to the present age and the ascendency of Hillary Rodham Clinton. Willow thought Republicans were incapable of compassion, that they just couldn't help it, they were just born that way, and that she and her fellow Dems were there to help the GOP do what it couldn't do for itself.

And rest assured that the words "Bush" and "Trump," were never spoken, only spat.

This Willow was dating a Republican?

I started a list on a tablet next to the Cheetos. "Republican," I wrote as the first item. I had a feeling I was going to have to carefully suggest that Willow do some of her own research. Of course, that would mean I would have to explain Google again, but I could take that on if it meant that she'd have a bigger picture of who this guy really was.

I wrote my next question under Beau's party affiliation: "Consultant of what?" I searched Beau's company's website and found only vague references to "helping clients live the way they deserve," and "finding peace at every part of the journey." I couldn't tell if Beau was hawking yoga classes or providing mortician services. I underlined my words and added another question mark.

Facebook was next. I'd accepted Beau's friend request when he sent it after our dinner at Chef Paolo's. Since Beau was making his page available to me, I didn't expect to find a lot of good dirt that he wouldn't want Willow's good friend to know. I completely ignored the top page and scrolled down as far as I could until I had the option of looking at previous years. I clicked on the first year Beau joined Facebook, five years earlier, and found lots of posts that, when combined, could have been published as a *Chicken Soup for the Wounded Soul.* Lots of blather about pressing on, how the trial wouldn't consume him, how when people were unfair and unkind, you could just light some incense and take that burning stick of incense with you as you took a walk in the hills wearing *lederhose*n and a felt hat. I'm paraphrasing here. Okay, fine, maybe there weren't any references to *lederhosen.*

I started cross-referencing some of the names that had "liked" such posts. Who were the people who wanted Beau to get through whatever he was enduring? Who wanted him to burn that incense and remember to be strong and memorize all the words to "Wind Beneath My Wings?"

One woman recurred. Her name was Jill Armstrong Beckley and her page was private. She rarely commented other than the occasional smiley face or broken heart but she had liked every single one of Beau's posts during the entire incense phase. Her presence dwindled to nothing after about a year, but for that year of sappy posts, Jill Armstrong Beckley must have been an important person in Beau's life. I wrote her name on my list and looked at the clock. An hour until school pickup and I had one more place to check.

In the age of Internet stalker weirdos (not including me, of course), Beau's eHarmony's page was private. However, eHarmony assured me every forty-five seconds that I was perfectly welcome to start my free trial and begin the rich and satisfying journey of finding the love of my life. After the sixth prompt, I started filling in information. I figured only a finite number of men would have checked "Springdale" as a possible match location, so I thought I'd likely be able to view Beau's profile at some point in the process. I entered the information, noting I was having a little too much fun and should probably stop reading fiction for awhile.

Name: Lizzie

Occupation: Librarian (toned down after I initially wrote my other dream profession, Cirque de Soleil performer, considering what kind of man would be interested in those kinds of skills.)

Age: 45

Religion: Christian (I assumed Willow had said as much as her faith ran deep and beautiful in her. Also, I really didn't have it in me to wade through profiles of all the Wiccans in the area.)

Finding a profile photo was an adventure unto itself. I needed to find an image that was not of anyone famous but that was pretty stinking beautiful, because, come on. If I had to relinquish Cirque de Soleil, I was going down with a fight. I found that, after about a page and half of image searches on Google, the results got absolutely bizarre. In addition to lots of cleavage and piercings, page three of my search for "middle aged brunette" yielded a Crock Pot, a kitten dressed in a woodchuck costume, and a lovely montage of the Black Hills of South Dakota.

After considerable wading, I found her. Or me, as it were. I looked great for my age. Soft chestnut waves framing a face that had a few smile wrinkles and a smattering of freckles on my nose. I'd always wanted freckles. Bright and inquisitive blue-gray eyes and the eyelashes I'd coveted since seeing the full, Maybelline version of Tawnie Edwards's lashes in sixth grade. My eHarmony eyelashes were way better than Tawnie's *and* I had a job and a cute one-and-a-half–story Arts and Crafts bungalow with a spacious porch and well-tended gardens and a reading nook and a brick driveway and a recently renovated kitchen.

Right.

See what I mean about needing to lay off the fiction?

The final bell would ring in fifteen minutes, so I needed to leave on my walk to Nora's school. I closed the Google window and logged out of Facebook. When I went to close out of eHarmony there were nine new notifications in my inbox. The first matches. Wow, I thought. These people were serious about me getting after it and finding true love. I scrolled past Dan from Prior Lake with red hair who played Ultimate Frisbee and loved cats, making a mental note to go into my profile and clarify that I hated cats. Past Tom from Burnsville who had an unfortunate set of braces. Past Ryan from Anoka who liked to knit. I didn't really want to think about Ryan knitting.

And there he was. BVaughn from Minneapolis. I smirked at the profile photo. A little indulgent, I thought. It was Beau From A Decade Ago. Same great hair, only more black than gray. Same great smile only not one wrinkle in the smooth skin surrounding it. His eyes looked different somehow but I chalked that up to the use of a black-and-white photo. I narrowed my eyes as I skimmed his profile. Everything checked out to what I already knew, and I could see why Willow had agreed to contact Beau. What woman would deny the chance to meet a man who liked making his own pasta on the weekends, loved good wine but loved sharing it with someone during a sunset picnic even more, and who said that travel, and I quote, "opened doors and windows to the adventure-starved soul"? Lizzie with the great eyelashes certainly couldn't miss her chance and before I could talk Lizzie/myself out of it, I clicked on the prompt to let BVaughn know that if he so chose, he could e-mail me at a brand spanking new, fake e-mail address.

I shut my laptop and paused, hands spread across the smooth gray surface. A twinge of guilt made its way into my thoughts and settled in my stomach. Was I wrong to be doing this underground research? Should I have just talked to Willow or, better yet, Beau, given him the chance to answer my nagging questions about the inconsistencies in his story?

I would, I decided, sliding the laptop to the couch and slipping into my shoes as I hurried onto our front sidewalk. I started to jog, hearing the bell ring outside the school and knowing Nora would be looking for me soon. I would talk with Beau, the very next opportunity that arose. The Internet searches and eHarmony info would just allow me to be more specific, to be less feeling-based in my questions and more fact-based. Why did he fudge his responses on whether or not he had lived in a small town after college, for example? Why were nearly all his business clients women, this after Paolo had mentioned the parade of beautiful women on Beau's arm throughout the years? What *was* his business, anyway? And why was his eHarmony profile pic so misleading? The fact that I had just posted a photo and backstory of a woman who didn't even exist was beside the point. I *had* to be a liar. It was my job. And while I was sure no small amount of filtering and airbrushing had made its way to the eHarmony experience, I thought it odd that a dude would be so vain as to erase all his wrinkles and pretend like the last decade of aging hadn't even happened.

I rounded the corner and waved to Nora, who was standing in her polka dot dress and knee socks under our maple tree. Weaving through the throng of kids and parents and barely escaping with my life after an angry carpool driver swerved around a staller, I decided I was doing the right thing by Willow. Willow was my friend and I was doing a kind of research she never would, all in an effort to protect her. Maybe Beau was who he said he was. Maybe this was all just a misguided intuition and Beau would come out squeaky clean. But as I scooped Nora up into a hug and shouldered her backpack as we set off, I knew I at least had to try and find out.

14

Jake pulled the car to a slow stop and I could feel him tensing beside me.

"Right," I said into the phone. I met his gaze and tried to convey I was almost done talking with Annie. "It can be crazy to share your body with a growing, living thing. It's totally normal that you're craving cheddar cheese and popcorn and that you cried about the cheese not melting fast enough."

I rolled my eyes at Jake, but he didn't even try to smile. He pointed to the clock on his phone and then to the building before us. I nodded again.

"You okay?" I said to Annie, still hearing the intermittent sniffle. "Go tell James he can't say things like childbearing hips anymore, no matter if he thinks it's a compliment. I'll call you tomorrow. And one of these days we need start talking about your baby shower. Maybe we can even work up a registry at LaSalle's Market and you can ask for blocks of cheddar."

She laughed and we signed off. I turned to my husband. "I'm sorry. Annie's having a tough time and I didn't know how to cut her off."

Jake's hands gripped the steering wheel though the car was still and we heard only the clicking of the engine as it cooled.

"I'd wanted to talk about our questions for Moira before we got here."

I stared at the Victorian house in front of me. It had been converted to a business years ago, but Hope's Reach had been the organization to bring it back to its former beauty. Every board and piece of trim was painted with care, every spindle and post on a yawning porch pretty and clean. The grounds were simple but tidy. Boxwood bushes formed a green symmetry in front of the porch railing, dotted with the last blooms of rose bushes and a smattering of plum-hued chrysanthemums. The front door was a beauty of etched glass and polished oak.

I took a deep breath and let it out slowly.

"And for the record," Jake said more gently, "you don't have to give Annie her baby shower. Let her mom and sisters do that."

My voice sounded far away, even in the sound bubble of Jake's car. "I'm fine. It will be fine."

Jake looked like he wanted to reply but he said nothing. He reached for his door handle. "We'd better go in. It's time."

I watched as he walked to the front sidewalk, hands in his pockets, scowling a bit at the house before him. I knew without asking that he was wondering who had done the paint job and if they'd used Elliott Paints. I felt a lump form in my throat, and I swallowed hard. Jake's scowl did nothing to mask how much he wanted this meeting. And my unwillingness to get off the phone with Annie and her cheddar dilemma did nothing to mask how much I felt conflicted about this meeting. I got out of the car and walked to meet Jake on the porch. He reached over to ring the bell. He took my hand as we watched the light and colors shift behind the glass as someone moved toward the door.

Moira herself showed us in. She was petite and compact and somehow conveyed even in the way she opened the door that she was energy waiting to be unleashed. Her hair was cropped very short and was the kind of hairstyle I always envied because I wanted to spend less time wrestling with my own. After one failed attempt just after college, however, I could attest that the hairstyle that made Moira look like an enchanted fairy who also taught yoga would make me look like a tenured PE teacher named Madge.

"Welcome, Jake and Heidi. Please, come in." She opened her hand to the foyer and we stepped over the threshold into a spacious entryway that had a carved staircase as its focal point. A sitting room opened to the left, filled with western light during that hour of the afternoon. We followed Moira to the right, into her front office, which I supposed must have long ago been the home's dining room. Tall ceilings nudged my eye upward to crown molding and a painted medallion circling a muted brass chandelier. The room was comfortable and pleasantly worn, from the velvet upholstered chairs Moira offered us to the soft colors in the rug underneath our feet.

Moira sat behind a large desk that looked like it might have been built around the time construction began on the house. This desk was *old*. Stately and imposing, the surface of the desk was polished to a shine but the entire piece of furniture listed to one side as Moira lay her elbows on the tabletop.

She rolled her eyes. "This desk. I would dump it for an IKEA substitute in a second but it's protected by the endowment. So hands off."

I must have registered surprise on my face because Moira laughed.

"Sorry," she said, her dark brown eyes shining. "I've always had a hard time with the old internal censor." She grinned. "I know it's a great house and I do love it. I love the warp in the leaded glass windows even though I can't tell if the mail carrier is on the porch or the UPS man or someone wearing a costume to look like a member of the Village People."

Jake chuckled.

"I love the creak of the floorboards even though that means my colleagues can hear me pacing, which I do with great regularity." She shrugged. "And I love the quaint bathroom with its child-sized sink and original finishes, even though sometimes I feel like I'm doing some sort of dance routine to organize fitting myself in the bathroom and shutting the door, all without losing a limb."

My eyes widened. "You're not exactly a large woman, so this bathroom must be something out of a Roald Dahl novel."

Her eyes lit up and she clapped her hands. "Roald Dahl! Exactly! I am the BFG in this scenario!"

On an ambitious day, Moira may have been five feet two with stilettos and a lot of hair product. She looked positively diminutive behind the large desk. She shook her head as she began rifling through a stack of papers before her. "I loved the BFG," she said. "My father, who was about as tall as I and most certainly not a Big Friendly Giant, had such a knack for reading in magnificent British voices." She found the paper she was seeking and pushed the others to the side.

I decided I liked Moira Kapoor. Even with the knots in my stomach and the pounding of my heart to be doing what we were doing, Moira Kapoor seemed like the person I would want on my team.

"Now," she said kindly. "To the business at hand. I hear you are considering adoption."

I looked to Jake, who sat in the chair next to me and was sitting as ramrod straight as I was. We looked like two fifteen-year-olds interviewing for our first summer jobs at the Tastee-Freez. For my part, I felt the same nerves, the same ridiculous hope to impress, and the same disbelief that I had come to this point in adulthood.

"Yes. Right. We are considering it. Adoption, I mean." Jake was stuttering. Jake was not typically a stutterer. I wondered if stuttering was an automatic disqualifier for an adoptive couple, and didn't know if I would be crushed or relieved if it were.

Moira, to her credit as a human being, pretended not to notice that Jake couldn't put a subject and verb together in the same sentence. "Wonderful. I know you must have lots of questions at this point. Perhaps it would be helpful for me to give you a rundown of the process? And you can pipe up with questions as they occur to you?"

Jake agreed and I nodded my assent. I knew from all the printer paper Jake had used and the red eyes he'd sported by bedtime each night that he had done hours of research and reading about "the process." He didn't need a rundown. But I did and I leaned forward slightly to listen as Moira began.

"Hope's Reach is the oldest adoption agency in Springdale. We will celebrate our fortieth anniversary next year. We coordinate the placement of children born within the surrounding one hundred miles or so, and we work only with domestic adoptions."

"Why domestic?" Jake asked. "I've read about the millions of children in other countries who need homes."

Moira nodded, her dangly earrings catching the light. "Absolutely. I believe the most recent number is 150 million children worldwide who are orphans, abandoned, or otherwise in need of adoptive parents. The need is really overwhelming. Jake, you ask an important question. International adoption is incredibly important. Children who are abandoned or orphaned overseas often face insurmountable obstacles of poverty, human slavery, sex trafficking, lack of education. Things we can't even really conceptualize here in this pretty room." Her smile was sad. She shook her head. "Honestly, some days I feel like we are just putting tiny Band-Aids over all the splintering wounds of a dam that has been broken for a long time and that will continue to be broken for a long time."

She took a deep breath before continuing. "But when I see a child placed into the arms of an adoptive mom or dad for the very first time, I know that for that child, no matter the place on a map where he or she was born, a Band-Aid doesn't even begin to describe it. It's so much more than a fix. It's a home filled with love. It's being pursued and wanted."

I felt my pulse racing. My hands were clammy as I listened to Moira.

"The question of international or domestic is a very personal one and I don't believe there is a correct choice, just an individual choice. Hope's Reach has a long history of domestic and we know how to do that well. However, if you decide to pursue an international adoption, I can point you to agencies we trust."

My mind was beginning to spin. I should have read more, I thought. I should have prepared. Every sentence coming from Moira was bringing up five new questions and I was having trouble keeping up. Jake was talking and I tried to tune in.

"Does Hope's Reach practice open or closed adoptions?" he asked.

Wow. Breaking out the fancy terminology. Jake sounded like he was on a public television panel and I was suddenly irritated with his superior knowledge, even though I had to acknowledge I, too, had access to the World Wide Web, and that I'd made a point to ignore his every effort to give me fancy terminology.

"All our adoptions are open adoptions," Moira said. "The option for closed adoptions is no longer available under state law."

"Open?" I croaked, before clearing my throat and willing my vocal chords to sound less like I'd been putting away two packs a day. "Sorry. Can you talk more about that?"

"Certainly," Moira said, her eyes kind. "An open adoption requires that the birth mother meet the adoptive parents prior to the adoption and that after the adoption, the parents maintain an open relationship between the child and the birth mother."

All sorts of red flags were jumping around in my thoughts. What, like we would have our baby but our baby wasn't really ever our baby? Would we have to ask the birth mother over for holidays? Request that she bring the rolls and a pie to Thanksgiving and then make sure the child sat next to her at the table?

"Now, this means all sorts of things to different families, depending on the situation," Moira continued. "Some families see the birth mother often, including her in the growth of the child on a regular basis. Other families exchange a yearly update through the mail and that's it. The relationship is entirely dependent on the couple and the birth mother and how they negotiate what each party needs and wants."

Jake and Moira continued on with the discussion, teasing out financial details (crazy expensive), the average wait time for placement (eighteen months to two years, which put me at about ancient when the baby would finally arrive at our house), and the online portfolio process (it involved a computer). But I was stuck. Stuck with a smile on my face and the occasional head nod, and stuck at the Thanksgiving table. How could I possibly share this child? How, after all this time, all this waiting, would I be able to invite someone else into this tenuous relationship? Even if we chose international, how could I know that somewhere another, unknown woman was connected to me in such a profound and intimate way? Would it be worse to know this woman or to ignore her existence from the moment we signed papers and got on a plane back to Springdale, busy with Little League and school supplies and trick-or-treating?

How would my heart grow big enough to survive all these things?

Moira looked at me and I had the distinct impression she was repeating a question. "Do you have any other questions at this point, Heidi?"

"*Hm*? No. Thank you. I'm fine," I answered as if she'd just offered me a refill of my Diet Coke, not the chance to quiz her on a child that would come to my home and be a part of our lives forever.

She looked thoughtful, eyes still on me. "You two go home, talk about this, think about it for a good long while. Let it steep. Adoption is not an easy road. It is beautiful and it completes puzzles that need to be completed for both parents and children. But it's not easy." She swallowed. "My husband and I have two adopted children, and when I watch your faces, I remember again the rawness of this conversation."

I blinked furiously. Jake took my hand.

"If you're like us, you've already been wanting a baby for a long time. After the exhausting road of infertility, couples are already spent. And while I'd like to tell you otherwise, the adoption process doesn't happen quickly. It's the longest pregnancy ever."

I was grateful she didn't make a quip about the absence of stretch marks or the chance to miss out on a hard labor. Oh, how I still wanted the stretch marks! What I wouldn't have given for a hard labor!

"We are praying people around here," Moira said as she rose from her chair. "We will start praying for you, Jake and Heidi Elliott, that God would make it clear if you are to adopt a child. He will be good to walk with you through this, whatever you decide."

We said our good-byes, promising to keep in touch. I squinted in the sun as we walked slowly to our car. Jake opened my door, and I slid into the passenger seat.

The air was full of questions and decisions and wonderings as Jake started the car. I opened my window and let in the damp fall air, or maybe I was trying to get the weighty air out.

"You want to talk?" Jake finally asked.

I sighed. "Yes, but not yet. Do you?"

He shook his head. "I need to think."

I nodded silently. The air from outside rushed over me and I closed my eyes to the sun, which suddenly felt intrusive. Yes, but not yet, I thought again. Just not yet.

15

Nora came running into our bedroom wearing absolutely nothing but a sombrero. That's not entirely true. She was also shaking a pair of red maracas. The white print on the maracas, I knew, read "¡Cabo San Lucas!" but Nora was shaking them with such fervor, all my eyes could register was a blur of red, white, and naked booty.

"Mom!" she said, still shaking. "I need your help!" She was full-on shouting above the racket of the maracas. The sombrero was roughly eighteen sizes too large for her head and kept slipping down over her eyebrows. She couldn't possibly, as Gloria Estefan would say, turn the beat around, so instead of relinquishing a hand to push the hat up onto her forehead, she kept tipping her head backward through the percussion solo. At the point of her questioning, her chin was pointed to the light fixture above our bed.

I finished wriggling into my favorite pair of jeans. God bless the person who persisted until finally creating jeans that had curves, tucks, and most importantly, just the right amount of Thank-You-Jesus Spandex so that a girl could still look cute in denim even if that girl wasn't an Eastern European lingerie model. I took one quick look in our full-length mirror and decided my outfit passed muster. Topping the jeans was an embroidered shirt I'd purchased in Mexico a few years ago. It had a pretty neckline, three-quarter-length sleeves, and a slight flare at the bottom. Fitted but not too fitted. One did not need to look like the dude on the beach who slept in a hammock and played Hacky Sack through a haze of Mary Jane just because one was wearing an embroidered shirt.

"Show me what you have so far," I said to Nora as she shimmied out of the bedroom toward her own room at the end of the hall.

"I have my hat and my shakers and my striped socks but that's it!" Nora's voice raised in pitch as she ticked off each item. She took off the sombrero and tossed it onto her bed. "I need more clothes to cover my body!"

I really, really, really wanted her to say that again and then type it up to have her sign it as a reminder of all that was good and true when she entered high school. But I tried to stay focused.

"Honey, you're doing great. We'll find something together." I turned to one of her open dresser drawers and began pawing through the mess of clothing. "This is supposed to fun, Peanut. Willow's house is always fun, right?"

Nora began hopping on one foot. The maracas shook with each hop. "I'm glad she is having a fiesta party. I've never been to a fiesta party."

I chuckled. Only Willow. She'd called early that morning, her speech hurried and excited, and asked if Jake, Nora, and I could make it to her house for dinner that evening. She was having a few people over for tacos and margaritas, she said, and could we please wear something Mexican-ish? I'd readily agreed, and only partly because Willow's cooking was always a draw and

I would love a night off in the kitchen. I was also excited to have Willow to myself. Even if I had to share her with a crowd of people, I knew Beau was out of town for business, and the mere thought of it made my shoulders relax. I was hoping to snag Willow away for a few minutes and talk with her about the meeting with Moira. I pictured the time after dinner while everyone else was chatting in the backyard, how I would steal her away to her little office lined that was with books, and how I would unload my heavy heart about adoption. She would know just what to say, just how to comfort, just the words to pray before we returned to the party.

I rummaged through Nora's clothes and heard myself sigh, so hungry for some Willow perspective about this whole thing. I hadn't even told her about the last miscarriage. I'd meant to talk about it during the Juniper Row lunch but once she'd confessed she'd met someone online, I never steered the conversation back to anything else.

I held up a long-sleeved T-shirt with flowers printed down the front. "How about this? This is tropical, right?"

Nora made gagging noises and I cursed again the choice to send her to school. The cafeteria chatter alone was a bad influence.

"That shirt is disgusting. And it doesn't match my maracas." She gave another shake for emphasis. Stopping suddenly, her eyes lit up. "I know what to wear!"

She ran to her closet and threw open the door. Down on her hands and knees, she tossed behind her one item of clothing after another until she emerged, victorious, holding up a very wrinkled, very floral, very forgotten sundress from at least two summers before.

"This is perfect!" she said, giddy. She smoothed the fabric

over her body to show me its perfection. The bottom hem, which had originally fallen to her ankles, now sat just below the knee. The bodice seemed comically small.

"Norie, that's a very pretty dress but I don't think you're going to be able to fit it any more. You wore that dress a long time ago and now you're a huge kindergartner. Plus," I said, walking toward her, "it's a summer dress. You'd be supercold. It's only fifty-five degrees outside." Only Willow, I thought. She'd promised heat lamps and a fire in the fire pit, but a fiesta in October? The woman had a penchant for bringing people (forcibly) together, if only to end up burning our shirts over an open fire to keep warm.

"I won't be cold." Nora's voice came out muffled as she began stuffing her arms through the bottom of the dress. "I can wear a sweater."

I crossed the room and helped her tug the dress over her head and shoulder blades. The scrunchy fabric did, in fact, give enough to stretch across her torso but it looked ridiculous.

"Nora," I began, turning back to the long-sleeved tee, "what about—"

"Ready?" Jake said as he entered the room. I could smell his aftershave and his hair was still wet from showering.

I pointed to his outfit. "Jeans and a Bruce Springsteen T-shirt?"

He grinned. "My favorite fiesta wear."

"Jake," I said, shaking my head, "we're supposed to wear something tropical. Something Mexican. You're wearing New Jersey."

"Come on," he said. Now I had two whiners in the same room. "Heidi, I hate costume parties. I feel ridiculous. Please don't make me wear Mexico. Please let me wear Bruce. He probably loves Mexico. He probably has a huge house in Mexico."

I looked at Jake, looked at Nora, who was accessorizing her postage stamp dress with a pair of sparkly play high heels, sombrero still slouching over her browline.

I sighed. "Let's get in the car."

✦   ✦   ✦

Willow met us at the door, a margarita in each hand. "For you and Jake. I saw the slow progress up the driveway and thought you might need these."

I rolled my eyes. "There's a reason five-year-olds don't wear high heels. Moral reasons, sure, but also because they can't exactly walk."

"I can walk! Watch!" Nora walked from the door to the stairs in Willow's entryway. Her hips swished side to side and her ankles gave out every other step.

Willow pulled me into a hug and I knew she was trying to hide her laughter from Nora.

"She looks like a ten-penny hooker with a drinking problem," I said into Willow's hair and she snorted.

"Hey, Willow," Jake said, taking his drink and his turn with a hug. "Thanks for having us. It smells phenomenal."

It did. I knew at once the night was going to be a raging culinary success because I could smell Willow's slow-roasted pork. I'd eaten that pork and still occasionally had really happy dreams about it. That baby had been in the oven, low and slow, all day, and the cumin, garlic, and beautiful aroma of pork filled the house. It made my mouth water just thinking of how it would fall into a heap, ready for us to spoon it onto corn tortillas with some of Willow's homemade salsa verde.

"Everyone's out back. Come," Willow said. She took Nora's hand. "Let's make an entrance." She matched Nora's sashay and the two giggled us through the house to Willow's backyard.

The sun had set but some twilight remained and mixed with the strings of lights Willow kept looped in her trees all year round. The patio sat two steps down from the house and I paused in the doorway to take in the elevated view. I saw lots of dear and familiar faces among the revelers. I glimpsed Willow's sons, the twins, Blue and Stream, and their older brother, Hike, all of whom I planned on hugging fiercely. They looked so grown up, now that they had graduated from college and had real jobs and haircuts. I waved to a group of women standing under one of the patio heat lamps and felt a rush of affection for them. These women were a part of a moms' group at our church, and they had walked patiently through the early, dicey years of parenting with me. I realized with a wince that it had been weeks, months even, since I'd attended a meeting. Our struggle with having a baby had ripple effects, and one of them was that a group devoted to motherhood hurt too much. I waved at Molly, Laura Ingalls, and Faith and promised myself I'd give it another try. Soon.

I took Jake's arm and stepped down to the patio. Exuberant Latin music played from a speaker somewhere and I was pulling Jake's ear down to me to say I was going to talk to the church girls when my heart sank. Beau was approaching us, crisp white linen shirt open at the collar and dark wash jeans stopping at a pair of leather and canvas flip-flops. His relaxed elegance was a far cry from plastic heels and Bruce Springsteen.

"Jake! Heidi! I'm so glad you could make it." He reached out to shake my husband's hand.

"Good to see you, Beau," Jake said, returning the handshake.

"I thought you were out of town on business," I blurted. Even I could hear the disappointment in my voice, so I rushed to employ the quick-smile as a cover-up.

Beau shrugged. He seemed oblivious to how I really felt. Quick-smile rides again!

"I was supposed to leave tonight but Willow got a wild hair to throw this shindig and, well." He shrugged again and laughed. "What can I say? She can be very persuasive."

Ew. I kept my face neutral and tried not to think about Willow's methods of persuasion.

Jake nodded toward the kitchen. "It wouldn't take much to get me to stick around for some of Willow's cooking. I'm pretty sure you wouldn't be eating like this on some airplane."

"True enough," Beau said, face alight. "I'm finding Willow is an improvement in pretty much every area of my life, including the avoidance of airplane food. Of course, I will eventually have to return to my real job."

Beau and Jake shared a laugh. I coaxed my face to relax from its Stepford Wife imitation. I tilted my head and formed my first question. "Speaking of your job, Beau," I said, "we'd love to hear more about what you do. What is it, exactly, that you do?"

Jake looked at me with a quizzical expression. I was not usually the person in the room asking people about their jobs. I was usually the person in the room organizing the mambo line. I avoided Jake's gaze and waited for Beau's response.

Beau waved away the annoyances of the work world, so far from Willow's charming background and the margarita he held in one hand. "Oh, it's not nearly exciting enough to talk about here. Numbers, data, you know. I could tell you more about it sometime. If you have absolutely *nothing* better to do."

He slapped Jake on the back as he laughed. The slap made

Jake jump but he recovered quickly and joined in the merriment.

"So numbers and data," I persisted. "Paulo said you brought a lot of clients—female ones, if I remember correctly—to his restaurant. Do the females talk about numbers and data too?"

Beau looked at me a moment, and I saw a flash of irritation cross his face before he corrected it. "Yes, I have certainly run up the business account at Paolo's. I don't really know the breakdown of whether I've hosted more women than men."

I cocked my head. "Really? *Hm.* I'd think you'd know that right off, what with being a numbers guy."

"Heidi," Jake said quietly.

Willow approached us and Beau's face registered unadulterated relief. I kept my eyes on him and could feel Jake's eyes on me.

"Hi," Willow said, shyly, only to Beau. She wrapped him in a hug and he whispered something in her ear. She laughed softly and turned to us without extricating herself from Beau's embrace.

"I'm afraid I have to snag this dreamboat," she said.

Beau rolled his eyes but his smile said anything but that he hated the moniker.

Willow took Beau's hand with both of hers and started walking backwards toward the house. "Almost time to eat and I need a sous-chef."

"I guess this means we'll have to finish our conversation later," Beau said, eyes on me. He turned toward Willow and kissed her on the cheek, then continued their joint progress toward the house.

"Jerk," I said aloud.

Jake used both of his hands to turn my shoulders to face him. "Heidi, what the heck was that all about?"

I wriggled free of his grasp. "Nothing. No, it is something." I sighed. "I've been doing some Internet research and I think Beau isn't who he says he is. I think he's hiding something."

Jake shook his head as if trying to clear it. "Wait, what? Internet research? Like Google?" He said the word as if he'd asked if I were running around asking questions of the Sewer People.

"Yes," I said, defensive. "Google. And other places."

"What other places?" Jake's eyes narrowed. "Do not say social media."

I chose to ignore what he was implying. My research was sound, dang it. "Okay," I said, numbering my finds with my fingers. "His company website is bizarre. I can't figure out what he does and why there are so many women involved."

Jake shrugged. "Lots of people have unclear websites. And lots of people are women."

I went on. "He went through some horrible time a few years ago and his Facebook page is full of sappy, sad memes and posts about perseverance under fire."

Jake's jaw dropped open. "Heidi. You are describing roughly one hundred percent of social media posts."

"Yes, but all his sappy memes were liked or commented on by one particular woman, a woman neither Willow nor Beau has ever mentioned. And after the sad and sappy time, her name just disappears from his posts."

Jake was rubbing his eyes.

"And here's the real sketchy part," I said hurriedly. I was losing him. "He keeps on playing up how he doesn't know anything about small town life, small town life is so charming, so different from the big city, yada yada." I leaned in, my eyes locked on Jake's. "But he *lived* in small town. Why does he keep ignoring that? What happened in that small town that he doesn't want to remember?"

Jake stared at me as if I had morphed into a cyclops before his very eyes. "Heidi," he said slowly. "You are insane."

I made a face and tried to speak but he clamped his hand over my mouth. Not just a finger to shush, an entire hand. Over my mouth.

He shook his head slowly. "I love you. So much. But I can't afford to have you committed to an institution. Not now. Let's wait until Nora graduates from high school and then we can talk about this again."

I peeled his hand off my mouth and scowled. "I know there's something off about this guy." I didn't mention my most compelling evidence, the fact that BVaughn was still an active account on eHarmony. Jake might not feel fantastic to know his own wife had just opened an account, even if his wife was faking her identity as Lizzie the Librarian.

Jake looked toward the house. He seemed lost in thought. When he turned to me his eyes looked suddenly mournful.

"Heidi, I get it," he said, emotion in his voice. "This is all hard. Wanting a baby is hard and thinking about adoption is hard and not getting the answer we want from God is very hard. Exhausting." He ran a hand over his face. "But it's not Beau."

I stiffened. "It's definitely Beau. I'm not even thinking about all that other stuff."

Jake's laugh was wry, weary. "Really? Because I'm thinking about it all the time. And I want to talk about it. With you." He tried taking my hand but I pulled away. I knew without looking the injured look in his eyes, and I didn't want to see it. I kept my gaze fixed on the string of lights just above us in Willow's Japanese maple.

Jake was silent for a long time. He finally cleared his throat.

His tone had hardened. "I'm trying to give you space and room. I really am. But the distance is growing, Heidi. And at some point, you need to close it."

Nora came bounding up, saving us from ourselves. I turned a full-wattage smile on her. Jake ruffled her hair and started walking toward the house. I could see in the set of his shoulders that I'd hurt him. No matter, I thought, acting like I was listening to Nora's story about how she had scored three sodas already, but really thinking about Jake's words. I'd figure out what was going on with Beau and then Jake would have to admit my hunch was right. And then we could talk about everything else. The everything else could wait.

Nora had come to the part in the story she seemed most excited about. "And then," she said, bouncing up and down, "I found a big metal thing full of ice!"

Wait. Three sodas? Who were the sadists in this backyard that had allowed this to happen? I scanned the yard and my gaze landed on the patio door where Beau was emerging with a fresh trash bag.

I cut Nora off. "I'll be right back, Peanut."

"But Mom!" she called after me. "I haven't told you about the chocolate-covered caramels!"

I beelined for Beau. He was alone, his back to me. It was time to get some answers and put this thing to rest.

He startled when I said his name. "Heidi," he said, not even trying to hide his displeasure. "Good grief, you scared me to death."

"Sorry," I said. "Listen, Beau, I think we need to talk. I have some questions."

"Okay," he said, straightening up from replacing the lid on the trash bin. "Shoot."

"Why are all your business clients women? I tried to figure it out on your website but I couldn't find an answer."

He sniffed. "You stalked my website?"

"No," I said in my best Room 12 singsong. *Actually, I stalked your social media and your eHarmony profile.* "I was just looking into what you did for a living. Just curious."

He didn't look convinced. "Well, it's complicated, Heidi. I do have male clients, but you're right. Most of my business is built to accommodate females." He paused. "You know," he said, crossing his arms over his chest. "I don't think this has anything to do with my business. I think you don't like me. And I can't figure out what I've done to make that happen."

I pulled myself up to my full height. "Beau," I began but didn't get a chance to defend myself because Willow was calling him from the steps leading to the house. She was waving him over. I was struck again by the new light in her face, the unadulterated happiness in her eyes. When I turned to Beau, he was mirroring her expression.

"I'm sorry, but we'll have to finish this in a bit," he said already striding toward Willow. "Don't worry. I won't forget." He winked at me. The smile on his face was playful and not one bit worried. He smiled like a man who knows he has the upper hand. I narrowed my eyes at him as he joined Willow on the steps leading to her house.

I was weaving my way back through the yard toward Jake and Nora, trying to get to them before Willow blessed the food and gave us dinner instructions. But Beau's voice was the one that rang out over the crowd.

"Thanks for coming, everyone. Willow and I are so happy you could make it on such short notice."

I caught the eye of Hike, Willow's eldest, and he wiggled his eyebrows at me as if acknowledging some sort of conspiracy. I furrowed my brow, trying to ask without words what he meant.

It would become clear soon enough.

"Listen, um," Beau said, and I could hear nerves in his voice, something new to my ears. "Willow and I want you to know that we really appreciate each one of you and your friendship. I'm only starting to get to know you all but I can already see why Willow loves you and what a great family she has in you."

I reached Jake. He kept his eyes fixed on Beau.

"So I'm hoping you'll be as excited as we are because, um, I've asked Willow to marry me."

"I said yes!" Willow said, clasping her hands, her face alight with joy.

The crowd whooped and hollered, raising their glasses and cheering as Beau and Willow kissed. I saw Hike, Blue, and Stream shaking hands with those around them and understood why they'd made an effort to come home so quickly, why Hike had looked at me with a glimmer in his eye, how he'd assumed that I knew.

I hadn't known. Willow hadn't told me.

I clapped along with the rest of the crowd but felt tears stinging my eyes. Nora was jumping up and down in her heels, and I didn't even warn her to be careful not to twist her ankle in the grass. Molly from our moms' group gave me a thumbs-up from across the yard. Her face softened when she saw the tears in my eyes. She thought I was moved to tears because I was so happy for my friend. I nodded, kept nodding when Willow caught my eye. Her face was tear-stained, her mascara starting to run.

"Let's eat!" Beau boomed from beside her. "She said yes!"

Jake scooped Nora up in his arms. "Come on, squirt. Let's give those feet a break. I'll carry you to the food." He looked at my face. "You okay?"

I tried my best quick-smile on my husband and could see he wasn't fooled. I walked slightly behind him as we entered the fray, following the music and the laughter and the news that things were definitely, irrevocably different.

✦ ✦ ✦

I was tucking Nora into bed, kissing her forehead and watching her eyes finally droop after the steep descent of the sugar crash, when my phone vibrated in my back pocket. I rushed to silence it. Nora's eyes fluttered but she settled right back into sleep. I reached over to turn off her bedside lamp and tiptoed out of the room.

In the hallway outside her door, I swiped through to the new e-mail.

It was from BVaughn. He was so happy to "meet" Lizzie through her profile and was eager to start a conversation. How was my night, he wanted to know.

I looked over my shoulder, though I could hear Jake in the kitchen and I knew he wasn't near.

How was my night? I felt sick to my stomach. Approaching another woman on the same night as his own engagement party. The *nerve*.

Oh, Willow.

I stood there a moment, holding the phone in my hand, staring at the e-mail. Tucking it back into my pocket, I set my jaw.

It was time to break up an engagement.

16

The following morning was a Saturday and because no part of life was fair, my daughter came into our bedroom just before six a.m. and put her face close to mine. I felt her nose touch my nose and I startled awake. Screwing up my face at the alarm clock, I moaned quietly when I realized the time.

"Nora, why are you awake?"

"Your breath is superduper stinky." She at least had the decency to whisper so she wouldn't wake Jake. Of course, her whisper was louder than most people at full voice, but she was trying.

"I know my breath is stinky. All breath is stinky at six a.m."

"Mine's not! Here. Smell." She unleashed a gust of hot breath on my face.

I tucked my nose under the sheet and said, "It's definitely stinky." My eyes were still closed in the hopes that Nora would see them in a state of sleepiness and would be inspired to pad back to her room and sleep for another three hours, just like I wanted to do.

Hot breath stayed, now diffused through the cotton sheet.

"Norie, honey, don't wake Mommy." Jake stirred as he whispered to Nora. "Go to the kitchen. I'll be there in a sec." He was already pushing off the covers.

"I'm up," I said around the frog in my throat. "Thanks anyway."

Nora skipped to the kitchen and I heard her opening the freezer. I knew this was an attempt to locate Saturday Morning Frozen Waffles. I groaned.

"What kind of human being can down three caffeinated sodas, roughly her weight in chocolate caramels, and two Costco churros in one night and not only bound out of bed an hour and a half *before* her normal waking hour but also seek out the nearest sugary breakfast on which she will pour synthetic Mrs. Butterworth's syrup?"

"Lots of words," Jake mumbled, clearly still half asleep.

I rolled toward him and formed my body to his, resting my head on his chest. I felt it rise and fall and took a deep breath of the fabric softener smell lingering on his shirt.

"Why aren't you superduper stinky in the morning?" I asked.

"Superduper tired. Can't be stinky and tired at the same time."

"You make absolutely no sense," I said, kissing his cheek, still warm from his pillow. "Go back to sleep. I'll deal with High Fructose." I sat up and began scooting to the edge of the bed when Jake pulled me back to him. He caught me in a close embrace and kissed me on the neck.

"Just because we fight about adoption all the time"—another neck kiss—"can't we still have sex?" Neck kiss, migrating-downward kiss.

I laughed. "We can still have sex. We'll just get really good at compartmentalizing."

"I'm a compartmentalizing genius," Jake said. His hands on the back of my neck made chills run up my spine.

"You are not," I said, shivering. "You're horrible at compartmentalizing. I'm the one who is awesome at it. I can teach you."

"Ooh, I love it when you do your naughty teacher." He tugged my earlobe with his teeth.

"I've never done a naughty teacher. And don't ask me to wear a maid's uniform."

"Mixed metaphor," Jake murmured into my hair.

"Jake?"

"Mmm?"

"We have a daughter."

"No, we don't."

"She's in the kitchen."

"Nah."

"She's going to want orange juice in about twenty seconds."

"Too acidic. She'll be fine with water. She can reach the faucet."

"Jake?"

Any extra encouragement to part ways for the moment came with Nora's voice right next to the bed.

"Mommy, are you wrestling Daddy?" Nora sounded thrilled. "Can I wrestle too?"

"Whoa, ho, ho," Jake said. He took his hands away from where they were wandering and held them up in the air, as if Nora worked for the FBI. "We're all done wrestling. Totally done. Right, Mommy?"

I was giggling into my pillow. "Very done," I said, my voice muffled.

"Aw," Nora whined. "I'm really good at wrestling. I know how to pin people."

Jake whimpered a little so only I could hear. "I love pinning people," he said, also in a whine. "Well, really just one people. I love pinning *that* people."

I snorted into my pillow.

"Daddy," Nora said. She was pretending to jump rope and her hair lifted and fell in wild sprays. "I can't reach the orange juice."

"Got it," he said. He rolled back toward me and kissed me on my neck once more. He sighed a sigh that would have been right at home in the final season of *Downton Abbey*. "I can't remember why we decided to have children," he whispered into my ear. "They are irritating and needy and they interrupt wrestling."

"I believe it all started *with* the wrestling," I whispered back. "But I'm glad you brought it up so we can keep fighting about adoption. That feels more natural anyway."

Jake dragged himself out of bed and followed the jump-roping Nora to the kitchen.

I stared at the ceiling while I listened to Nora boss Jake around with how much OJ she wanted and which cup was her favorite. The man's patience was astounding, I thought again. I sat up slowly and rubbed the back of my neck with one hand.

We're trying, I thought. We're trying to make our way back to each other. I closed my eyes, holding on to that thought and that hope, hoping it wouldn't take long and that we would reach each other intact.

✦   ✦   ✦

Oh, how the mighty had fallen. By four that afternoon, all the sunshine and roses that had started our day had definitely left the building. Nora and I stood in the middle of her bedroom, mirroring each other with our scowls and our hands on hips.

"Nora, you can be a ninja warrior when you trick-or-treat tonight but you have to wear more clothes than what you have on right now. It's October in Minnesota. Shorts and bare legs are not practical."

"Mom," she said, somehow making that one syllable stretch for miles. "I *have* to wear shorts. I'll be doing sweet ninja moves and I can't show people my vagina!"

The thing about insisting on using correct anatomical terms was that then you had to hear them. It could be jarring.

I let out a slow, tortured breath. "You won't show anyone your vagina," I began again. This wasn't our first turn around this circle. "And if you want to wear shorts, that's fine. You just need to wear tights underneath."

Nora's eyes filled with tears. "You don't understand," she wailed, shaking her head back and forth. "I can't be a sparkly USA ninja warrior in *those tights.*" She pointed with an accusatory glance at the red tights lying deflated and rejected on her bed. "Those tights are ugly. And they aren't sparkly at all."

"You loved them when we bought them yesterday," I said in a voice that was inching upward and outward. "We talked and talked in the middle of the aisle at Target and you promised these were the right tights. And we agreed, remember? We agreed that this was the last piece of your costume and that we weren't going to buy anything else. Right?"

Jake entered the room. He wore a sour expression at odds with his clothing. From top to bottom, I took it in: white cotton headband, red, white, and blue hockey jersey, white shorts, blue running tights, knee-high socks pulled up over the tights, and red Converse sneakers. He looked like he should grab a basketball and start whistling the Harlem Globetrotters theme music, but he twisted his car keys in his hands, frowning.

"I thought we had what I needed to grill burgers but there's no propane in the tank. And I don't have buns. So."

"Sorry," I said, not sounding sorry. "I should have double-checked this morning." I was grateful I had a husband who liked to grill on weekends. I wasn't as grateful that I seemed to be the only one who knew where the grocery store was located and how to make a complete list before getting ready to cook.

"It's fine," he said tersely. "I'm just hungry. And we need to leave soon if we're going to trick-or-treat in a timely fashion, so I'm just going to run and get sandwiches from Al's Deli."

I lowered myself to Nora's bed. Normally I would have teased Jake about wanting to trick-or-treat "in a timely fashion," but I was exhausted. I'd foolishly planned on catching up on some household organizing that day, and when it became clear by noon that my day was planned for me, compliments of Nora, my mood began a long spiral downward. I looked at Nora, who was now writhing on the floor, crying and holding the sparkly wand we'd made out of a chopstick and a cutout star. Staying late at Willow's engagement party last night was turning out to be a colossal parenting error.

Willow was engaged. The thought pushed me further into my funk.

"Sandwiches sound good," I said, distractedly. "Thanks."

Jake nodded at the writhing child on the floor. "Everything going all right here?"

I heard his sarcasm and raised him. "Perfect. We're just about ready to audition for World's Best Mom and Daughter."

"No, we are not!" Nora wailed, starting into another bout of crying.

I wanted to drink heavily. In Burma. Where they didn't trick-or-treat.

I let myself fall back on Nora's bed and tried to summon the reserves to finish the tights conversation. I heard Jake open the front door, close the front door, and then open it again.

"Heidi," he called. "The mail came!"

I paused, then called back, "Okay. You can just leave it on the kitchen table."

"Come see the mail," Jake said, in a voice considerably friendlier than the one he used only moments before.

I sighed. Since when had the mail become an event? Did we get double coupons for Papa John's?

When I rounded the corner into the family room, Jake was grinning. He waved a white envelope and letter in his right hand. "We've been approved for a home visit."

I inhaled sharply. "What? I thought Moira told you to do the paperwork but that we'd have plenty of time to reconsider because it takes so long to get things moving."

"I know," Jake said, his eyes bright. "I can't believe it. But I've been praying about it and I don't know. I guess God just made things happen more quickly than normal."

Praying about it. I gulped, trying to keep a neutral expression. We'd agreed we would both pray but it looked like only Jake had upheld his part of the bargain. And it also looked like God was listening.

"Isn't this great?" Jake said. He glanced at my face and must have registered the conflict there, because he quickly added, "I mean, it's just a formality. We can still stop the process if we change our minds. But I've read it takes much longer than this to get approved. So at least we'll have this out of the way and we won't be waiting to check this box."

"Mommy!" Nora called from her room. She sounded a little like she'd just found out the apocalypse was about to begin. In

Springdale. In fourteen seconds.

Jake stared at me, hope all over his face.

"It's great," I said, willing my voice to be optimistic. "Really. I mean," I tucked my hair behind my ears, buying time, "I'm surprised. It's fast. But that's good, right? You think that's good?"

"Absolutely," Jake said. "Like I said, this is just a small step. But some couples have to wait on this step forever."

"Moooooommmmm!" Nora had just found out she and only she held the four-digit nuclear code. The situation was dire.

"I'd better go," I said, hooking my finger toward Nora's room.

Jake crossed the distance to me in two strides. He hugged me, lifting me off the floor a bit. "Don't worry. We're still going slow."

"We are?" My voice sounded small into his neck.

"We are." He let me go. Pulling back, I saw mischief in his eyes. "Besides, who says we'll pass? You know this means they'll have to visit. Us. Here."

We listened for a beat to Nora, who was now moaning the words, "I'm the worst ninja ever!" over and over in rhythm to the foot she was stomping on the wall.

"A valid point," I said.

Jake turned to leave and I heard him whistling as he shut the door.

17

I sat very still, even though the pew underneath my tush felt about as comfortable as a bed of nails. Pastor Smits was finishing the service with a prayer and I was biding my time, planning my exit strategy.

It was an odd thing, to feel isolated in a room full of people.

This sanctuary, this group of people had been a refuge for me many times. From the folks of First Lutheran I had received advice on parenting, examples for how to live the Christian life, meals when I was too sick to cook, hope for my future, and inspiration for how to be a woman who loved God and loved people. But all those lessons, all that help and hope seemed far away today. I'd kept all our struggles with infertility to myself, at first because I thought they were temporary and later because I just couldn't bear to talk about it. I'd walk by the nursery on Sunday mornings and fix my eyes somewhere else, somewhere that didn't have chubby cheeks and full lips and soft skin, all of which did not come home with me after the service. I'd skirt around the families with young children when I dropped off Nora at Sunday school, working to keep a pleasant expression on my face when everyone on God's green earth seemed to be either pregnant or newly postpartum and wearing a baby in a carrier or pushing a stroller through the crowded fellowship hall. Eyes ahead, beeline for our pew, plan exit strategy. Repeat.

And as for the moments after I had entered the quiet of the sanctuary, during the worship, the prayer, the sermon, the communion, that was the part that felt the strangest. I missed the way I would feel God's presence during church, how I could feel His Spirit nudging me during the sermon, pushing me closer to Him and farther away from my own selfishness, my own sin, my own misguided attempts at cleaning myself up for Him instead of letting Him do that work. I did not feel His presence any more. I felt alone and more than a little hacked off, and I sure wasn't going to tell Him that. He knew, I supposed, but we were at a standoff, God and I. I wasn't asking for His pity, but I couldn't fake it either. God didn't seem to hear all the weepy prayers I prayed for all those babies, and I wasn't about to go back to singing "Great Is Thy Faithfulness" and pretend like nothing happened.

I was startled out of my reverie when the piano started up, signaling the end of the service. Jake had already begun chatting with a gentleman in the row behind us, so I busied myself gathering my purse and coat. I kept my eyes down, having found that eye contact at this part of the morning was deadly. The exit strategy depended entirely on speed. I signaled to Jake that I would pick up Nora and meet him at the car. I'd made it halfway to the back doors of the sanctuary when Molly Langdon stepped in front of me, blocking my path.

"Not so fast, missy," she said, wagging one manicured nail in front of my face. "I've been trying to catch you for four Sundays and you've slipped out every single time before I had the chance." She pulled me into a tight hug, pressing my chin into her shoulder pad. I got a healthy whiff of her hairspray, which, judging by the height and width of Molly's hair, I could safely assume was extra firm hold.

She pulled back and sized me up. "How are you, Heidi Elliott? I miss you."

I smiled, and this one was genuine. Molly was the one who had pushed me (nearly literally) to join the moms' group when she'd led it years ago. She'd insisted I would like it and I'd insisted I would not. Turns out, Molly was right. I *had* liked it, I'd met fantastic women, including Willow, and I'd ended up meeting Jesus because of it. Molly, it turned out, was usually right.

"I miss you too," I said. "I've been busy. You know, with Nora and school starting." I trailed off, hoping Molly would give me a pass like most people would when I reminded them I was the mother of a young child. It was a like the golden ticket, having a young child and being busy. People usually started shelling out the pity at the thought, many of them remembering sleepless nights, dark circles under the eyes, the absence of any sort of alone time. I put on my best exhausted face.

Molly ignored it completely.

"I know you're busy, honey. We all are. Even those of us with tired lady parts and grown children. It never stops."

I winced at the reference to Molly's lady parts. She didn't appear to notice.

"I saw your tears at Willow's party," she said. Her eyebrows, perfectly plucked, arched above a healthy application of shadow and liner. "How are you doing with this? I know you two are very close and I know a new man in the mix has to change things, even if he's a wonderful man." She patted my arm and waited for a response.

"Oh, um, I am really happy for Willow," I said, a little

stunned that Molly wasn't fooled by my tears-of-joy bit at the party. I thought I'd crushed it. "She deserves to find happiness again, after all the pain and sorrow she's had to experience."

Molly waved away my platitudes with her hot pink acrylics. "Of course, she does. That's not the point. The point is that change is still hard, even when it's a change you know is for the best."

My thoughts spun to Hope's Reach and adoption and all the unknowns those changes represented. I had a sudden urge to spill it all to Molly, to cry on her shoulder pad, to ask her to help me wade through all this junk, all my feelings of hurt and betrayal by God and inadequacy as a woman who couldn't carry a baby.

Instead I swallowed hard. It was too much for me, too hard to open up that wound, too many words that wouldn't make a difference anyway. I was summoning another way to say I was fine, an art I'd perfected in the last few months, when Willow and Beau walked up to me and Molly. Their hands were laced together as if they'd always walked around First Lutheran as a pair. My throat constricted as I forced my mouth into a smile.

"Well, look who's here!" Molly reached out to hug Willow. "Beau, honey, I'm Molly. I met you at the engagement party."

Beau's laugh was rolling and deep. "I remember you, Molly. You're the kind of person who's tough to forget." He smiled at her, eyes already affectionate. "You have a way of welcoming an outsider."

Molly patted his arm. "Well, thank you, sweet man. I can see you're a charmer, which is entirely appropriate. Willow deserves to be charmed."

I watched Beau's expression, looking for any trace of pleasure at being the master charmer, the man who could fool fiancées and women's ministry coordinators who wore inappropriately large shoulder pads. Beau avoided my gaze and turned to Willow, who was asking Molly about her recent travels.

"Oh, well, you know I like to jet set," Molly said. "Bali was beautiful, though I did tire of sleeping in a hammock. It's not as great as it sounds, and I had a heck of a time getting my hair to cooperate in all that humidity. I prefer Costa Rica. Much closer to home, lovely beaches, and lovely people. *Buena gente*, right, Miss Spanish Teacher?"

It took me a moment to realize Molly was talking to me, both because I was no longer a Spanish teacher and because Molly's Spanish sounded identical to her English.

"*Sí*," I said, nodding. Beau looked on amused, and I waited for him to pour on the Spanish-speaking charm in addition to the regular version. He said nothing, though, and seemed content to watch this conversation unfold.

"Well, I'm sure Dan's been waiting in the car for twenty minutes." Molly hitched her purse higher on her shoulder. "When an introvert marries an extrovert, a couple has to figure out a system. Our system is for me to talk and for him to go read the paper in the car. It works out just fine, as long as I don't go too far into the dinner hour." Molly hugged Beau once more. "You got a good one," she said, chin tipped up to accommodate the height difference.

"I know," Beau said, eyes on Willow.

Molly pulled me and Willow into a group hug. "You girls go get some lunch soon, okay? It's going to be a busy time. You'll need to just get it on the calendar or it will slip though the cracks."

Willow smiled at me. "Good reminder, Molly. We'll do it."

"Sure," I said, trying to mirror Willow's calm and self-assuredness with Beau only an arm's length away. "We won't forget."

I begged off when Molly's hair was still in sight. Flashing the tag with Nora's name, I said I didn't want to keep her Sunday school teachers too long. Willow looked a little confused at my sudden departure, but I waved cheerily and strode toward the door.

Molly might have lapped up the charm, but I was officially at my limit.

✦ ✦ ✦

When we got home from church and were gathered around the table, munching on our grilled cheese and tomato soup, Jake met my gaze and I knew the question he was asking with his eyes. I nodded yes. We had discussed it last night and had decided now was time to let Nora know about the adoption possibility. The home visit was scheduled for the next evening, and Nora was not the type of child who would let a person with a clipboard just waltz in our house without a full interrogation and improvised ballet routine. We needed to give her warning, both because she deserved to know and because if we wanted any chance of pulling off a successful home visit, we needed her full cooperation.

Jake wiped the corners of his mouth with his napkin and cleared his throat. "So, Norie," he said, "remember how we've been praying for a baby sister or brother?"

Nora nodded. "Totes."

Jake made a face. "Totes? What is this, Disney Junior? Where did you pick up *totes* as an acceptable way to use the word *totally*?"

Nora shrugged. "For realzees."

Jake looked like he was about to toss his grilled cheese against the window. I fully understood the alarm caused by realizing one's daughter was being influenced by the hoard and that the kindergarten hoard seemed to have grown up a bit since our days in school, but now was not the time. I could see Jake was ready to launch into a tirade about respect, the evils of SnapChat (though Nora was not yet a participant), and Miley Cyrus (the girl hit a chord; Jake worked her seamlessly into every tirade. It was a gift.). I caught his eye and shook my head quickly.

"We have news on the baby front," I said.

Nora's eyes widened and she looked directly at my belly, which, I could attest, was growing by the moment but only because of the second grilled cheese I was stuffing into it. "Is there a baby in there? Right now? Is it eating grilled cheese and soup? Right this second?" By the time she finished her questioning, her voice had reached a pitch only dogs could hear.

Jake jumped in, no doubt worried this conversation was quickly spinning out of his control. A daughter intent on trying out for a spot on *Jessie* and a wife who could start sobbing at any moment when reminded of her empty uterus.

"No, Peanut," he said. "There is not a baby in Mommy's tummy. But we aren't giving up. We are looking into adopting a baby. Do you know what that means?"

Nora had just taken a bite that was far too big for a mouth containing only baby teeth. "Of course," she said through bread and cheese. "There's a kid in my class named Jonah and he's adopted. He was born in Vietnam. He's definitely the most handsome boy in Room 12."

Jake looked instantly horrified. "He is? I mean," he lowered his voice, trying for nonchalance, I assumed, but mostly looking pained, "Jonah is the most handsome, huh? Wow. That's interesting. To be handsome. In kindergarten. To you. My daughter."

Nora furrowed her brow at him. "Daddy, you sound super-weird. And you have a big, scary vein that is popping off your forehead. Maybe you should take a nap."

Oh, for the love. This conversation was going nowhere fast and I had four loads of laundry to do that afternoon. "Kiddo, we are starting the process to adopt a baby. We want to give a home and a family to a baby who doesn't have a home and family."

Nora appeared to be mulling this over. She took a long swig of milk and then pulled the back of her hand across her mouth to clear the white mustache that formed. I bit my tongue but made a mental note to go over napkin etiquette. Again.

"Is the baby going to be from Vietnam? Because I want to go to Vietnam. Jonah said he went there two times with his family and they have pretty beaches and really good chicken noodle soup. Hey!" Her eyes lit up as she scrambled onto her knees, making herself taller in her sudden excitement. "Let's go to Vietnam with Jonah! He can show us where our baby is!"

"Oh, wow." Jake was rubbing his face with his hands and muttering. "Just what we need. International, overnight travel with the most handsome boy in the class. Didn't anyone here see *Spring Break*?"

I made a face. "Um, no. And I would never admit again that you have."

Nora was starting to bounce in her chair. "Should I call Jonah on your cell phone, Mom? His phone number is in the school directory. His last name is spelled B-E-E-C-H. He has really long eyelashes."

Jake groaned.

"Norie, honey," I said, trying to get the train back on the tracks, "the baby we adopt will be from around here. There are so, so many babies in the world who need homes, but we can't help them all. We can just help one."

Jake recovered enough to speak. "We want to know the baby's family and it's easier to do that if the baby lives here in the United States."

Nora nodded solemnly. "By the dawn's early light."

Jake's mouth dropped open but I pressed on. "Exactly. So this will take a very, very long time. We want you to know what's going on but this is kind of like Christmas. You know how long it takes for Christmas to get here?"

Nora rolled her eyes. "Forever and ever and ever. As long as my birthday."

"Right," I said. "So this is going to feel like that. But we wanted you to know because you're a part of this family."

"A great part," Jake said as he pulled Nora's chair toward him and then her wiggling body onto his lap. "Really, the best part, other than Mommy. Mommy's really pretty fantastic. And pretty. And brave." Jake looked long at me but I averted my gaze, feeling the exact opposite of brave.

"So the first tiny step of this whole thing is this week," I said, standing and beginning to clear the plates from the table. "A nice lady will come to our house and watch us hang out."

"Huh?" Nora said, looking like she'd misheard. "That sounds horrible."

She had a point.

"It won't be," Jake said quickly. "It will be totally fine. We can just act like she isn't there. Just be ourselves."

Nora made a face. "She's going to be in the room and I have to ignore her? Like when Gus Hill pulls a card and Ms. Charm tells us to ignore him?"

"Not exactly," Jake said. "The lady won't be in trouble. She just wants to watch our family and how it works. She has to make sure we are a safe place for a baby to live."

Nora looked doubtful. "Well," she said slowly. "That's going to be tricky. We have lots and lots of scissors."

I bit back a smile and took the first load of plates to the kitchen. I let Jake field the questions about scissors, then knives, then broken glass, then permanent markers. The warm water ran over my fingers and into the sink and I felt my heart continue to beat hard in my chest. I'd been better at convincing Nora that we were ready to adopt than I was at convincing myself. Parenting required lots of skills, but as I dunked a bowl into the soapy water, I thought my skill as Master Pretender might have been my most useful yet.

18

Monday mornings were always a bit of a shocker. The amount of mess that could accumulate in a dwelling after two days of three people running amok within it—well, let's just say I spent a good fifteen minutes every Monday morning standing still in the middle of the house, marveling at what slobs we Elliotts were. Strike that. What slobs *certain* Elliotts were. I loved my husband but I did not marry him for his cleanliness. Jake's desk at work was a picture of tidiness. In fact, sometimes I would mess with him when I visited the store and I would rotate his coffee mug a quarter turn, just to watch his face when he realized it was out of place.

Our house was a different story.

At home, I could track where Jake had been by the detritus he left behind. Pile of newspapers by the bed, except for the Sunday sports section, which I found next to the coffeemaker. Coffee grounds trailed to the sink, where I found the empty envelope for a water bill. The bill itself was on his desk in our home office, which was nothing short of an active land mine, but this was not my first rodeo and I could see that he'd rummaged in the top drawer for stamps, coming up with three empty sleeves.

And so it went.

As I said, I loved him. And love kept me there but it didn't keep me any less cranky about the mess.

By eleven o'clock, I had things mostly back in order, including a sparkly bathroom, another room where, ahem, I could see where Jake had been. Tonight was our home visit, and I wanted our house to look clean and put-together and all the things I didn't feel. I dropped onto the couch and surveyed my work.

It looked great, I decided, my gaze lingering over the shining kitchen countertops and wood floors so clean, they gleamed like the ones in commercials. I felt suddenly very weary and rewarded myself for my efforts by reaching into Nora's plastic orange Halloween pumpkin. The USA Ninjas had performed admirably during trick-or-treat night and had come back with one sore back from too many "sweet moves" (Jake) and an obscene haul of candy (Nora). I figured it was my duty as her mother to prevent both childhood obesity and tooth decay, so I'd been helping myself, particularly to the Snickers and the Butterfingers. Nora hadn't yet reached the phase when she would make a written inventory of her candy and threaten execution of any thieves. We were living in the Golden Age and I was taking advantage of it.

I reached for my phone as I started to nibble the edges of a peanut butter cup. Facebook was open and I saw I had two new friend notifications. One was a request from Donny Nimmers, a boy from my high school who, judging from his profile photo, had developed a penchant for self-tanning. Donny had not had three words for me the entire four years of high school, and I rolled my eyes as I clicked to accept his friend request. I really needed to start using healthy boundaries in my Facebook life, and it needed to start with self-tanners who were most certainly not "friends."

The second notification made me sit up straight and gulp down the rest of the peanut butter cup. No longer able to fault Donny Nimmers for his shot in the dark, I saw my own shot in the dark had come to fruition. Jill Armstrong Beckley, the woman who had plenty of comments and comfort to offer Beau during his dark night of the soul, had accepted my friend request. I'd sent it on a lark that first time I'd perused Beau's page, assuming she'd do as I did when I received friend requests from people with no mutual acquaintance and who I assumed were actually contacting me from damp, chilly basements in the Ukraine. But Jill had said yes. I quickly accepted, and before I could think myself out of it, I sent her a personal message.

Hi, Jill. I think we might know the same person. Beau Vaughn?

I waited. I could see Jill had Facebook open as well, but that could mean she always had it open and might not actually look at it for days. Just when I was about to gather my empty candy wrappers and start in on cutting out construction paper leaves for Ms. Charm, my phone vibrated. It was a message from Jill.

I definitely know Beau, hahaha. How do you know him? Is he on the prowl again?

My heart thumped so hard, I thought I could see it through my shirt. I typed a quick response.

He sure is. Do you mind if I ask you a few questions about him?

I didn't have to wait ten full seconds for her response.

Ask away! Hahaha! We'll have to meet in person. My lawyer said I can't blab stuff on Facebook anymore. Hahaha! I'm free right now, if you want to stop by.

Wait, what? My thoughts were reeling. Meet in person? Her lawyer? Right now? I stared at the address Jill had sent. It was in a town called Copper Grove, which was about forty minutes north of Springdale. My fingers hovered above my phone's keyboard, weighing the options. The home visit was scheduled to begin at 4:00 pm, a half hour after Nora got out of school. I might need that half hour in travel time but if I asked Jake to pick up Nora because I was running an errand . . . I typed quickly before I could talk myself out of it.

I'll be there in an hour. See you soon!

✦   ✦   ✦

"Good gravy," I said aloud as I pulled into Jill's housing development just under an hour later. My beat-up Honda Civic and I looked distinctly out of place. I craned my neck to see upward as I passed the mammoth houses on either side of Cedarwood Drive. I was fairly certain I could fit our entire house in the garages of some of those structures, and when I pulled into the circular driveway of 543, I just kept driving, entering the street once again. I idled at the bottom, asking myself for the fifteenth time after leaving Springdale if I was doing the right thing. I jumped when my phone rang out in the quiet car.

Willow.

"Hi, there," I said into the phone, instantly kicking myself for having answered. There might never have been a more appropriate time for voice mail, and I'd squandered it. "How's it going?" I hoped I sounded chipper.

"Great," Willow said. She sounded a little out of breath. "Well, that's not quite true. I'm on my way to pick out a wedding dress and it's stressing me out. I haven't exactly done this for awhile."

"I'm sure you'll do great," I said, distractedly. I thought I saw a figure at the door of 543. The clock on my phone said I had two minutes to get to the front door or I'd be late. "Where are you going to shop?"

"Oh, Dunham's. Maybe Sylvia's Bridal, though that seems a little much. It's not as if I'm the target market for the strapless bodice or a mermaid cut." She laughed and I could hear she was nervous.

"Hey," she said in a way that did not sound spontaneous but was meant to. "Are you free? Could you meet me downtown for a while? You know, just to give your honest opinion when I fall in love with something that looks like a gunnysack and the salesperson doesn't have the heart to tell me?"

I felt a pang of guilt in my chest. "I'd love to, Willow, I would, but I'm actually not in town right now."

"Not in town? Where are you?"

Scramble, scramble, scramble. "I'm, um, in Pierce. Picking up some things for Jake. For the store." The web was getting more tangled by the minute.

"Oh. I see." Willow didn't hide her disappointment well. "Well, that's okay. I probably won't find anything first time out anyway. And I'm probably freaking out for nothing. It's just a dress. The important part of the day is Beau, and I know he'll be there, even if I'm in a gunnysack." I could hear her talking herself down from the cliff, and I felt my stomach tighten to think of where I was and what I was doing.

"Right," I said, suddenly wanting desperately to end the conversation. "Well, I need to let you go. Duty calls!" I sounded ridiculous but the charade was killing me and I needed it to stop.

"All right," Willow said. "I'll call you later and we can set up that lunch we talked about on Sunday. Don't want to get Molly on our case." I could hear the smile in her voice but it sounded a little sad too.

"Sounds good," I said. "Good luck with the dress."

I hung up and felt just a little lower than a snake. Letting my forehead drop to the steering wheel, I entertained second, third, and fourth thoughts. What was I doing? I twisted around to see the house with the circular drive, pondering what I might find within. I pictured Willow, her face alight with happiness as Beau draped his arm around her during their engagement announcement. Willow, who deserved so much happiness and joy after all the grief she'd endured. Willow, who was so trusting of others, who assumed the best and didn't even watch the evening news anymore because she said it made her lock her doors and no one needed to lock a door in Springdale.

Willow, who needed someone to find out the truth before it was too late.

I lifted my head off the steering wheel and reached for the handle on my car door. I turned off the ringer on my phone and let the door shut behind me. Willow needs to know, I thought as I reached the towering front door of 543, and someone needs to have the guts to find out.

The doorbell hadn't even completed its long and complicated chime before I heard a series of numbers being punched into a keypad and the door swung open.

"Come on in," Jill said by way of introduction. She sized me up as I stepped into the dramatic foyer. "Wow. Beau's going younger and younger." She arched an eyebrow but her forehead was so free of wrinkles, nothing much happened. I suspected this was unnatural and very expensive.

"Oh, um, Beau and I aren't, um . . ." I was stammering. I thrust out my hand. "Heidi. Thanks for meeting with me."

She took my hand and gave it a limp shake. "No problem. Beau's one of my very favorite conversational topics." I could hear the bite in her words. I followed her as she led me through the foyer to a sunny, ornate living room. I tried not to focus on it, but Jill had sequins on her butt. She wore a hot pink warm-up suit, and by hot, I mean brighter than the sun's surface. If Nora knew that clothing existed in that color, I would have to invest in retina-protective eyewear. Across the rump of her pants, Jill had the word "TASTY" written in silver sequins. Despite her efforts with her dermatologist, I was fairly certain that Jill was Willow's contemporary, probably pushing fifty years of age. I didn't want to be an ageist, but I was sure no butt of that vintage, or any vintage for that matter, needed to pronounce itself tasty.

"Can I get you a drink?" Jill asked as she walked to a fully loaded liquor cart. Lines of crystal decanters stood sentry for Jill's use and judging by the generous splashes she put into her glass, Jill's use was frequent.

"No, thank you. I had a healthy injection of coffee at breakfast." Which was only two hours ago, I thought to mention but did not.

Tasty Tush pointed to a sprawling white sectional. "Suit yourself. Let's sit."

I sat and folded my hands on my lap, feeling awkward. I crossed and then uncrossed my legs, cleared my throat. Jill seemed not to notice any of my discomfort as she was preoccupied with stirring the ice cubes in her lowball.

She looked over her glass. "So you're porking Beau."

I had just inhaled and the shock of those words made me choke on air or spit or the complete ludicrousness of the question. Either way, Jill rose languidly from her spot on the couch and started pounding me on the back until I stopped coughing.

"Thank you," I squeaked and she gave another three hard whacks before returning to her seat.

"No prob," she said and took a healthy swig of the amber liquid that had never left her hand, even during the whacking.

"I'm not actually, um, dating Beau. But one of my best friends is. They're engaged."

Jill snorted her laughter. "Oh, that's rich. All his talk about not ever getting married again. Whatever." She shook her head. "Just add it to the list of lies."

My stomach was starting to turn. "How do you know Beau? I only found you because of your comments on his Facebook posts, but I don't know how you two are connected."

Jill's eyes got large under her false eyelashes and heavy black liner. "We were married for twenty-four years. We have two children together. We built this house together." She made a wide arc with one arm to the space around us. "That's how we are 'connected.'" She said the word as if it implied a nasty skin affliction.

Married for twenty-four years. I gulped. Jill was Beau's ex-wife. His amicably divorced ex-wife, according to him. I searched her face for anything amicable and came up empty.

Jill seemed like she was the kind of girl who could handle a straight shot, in more ways than one, as it happened. So I shot straight.

"What happened?"

She shrugged. "He left me. High and dry after twenty-four years together, twenty-six if you count the years we dated."

I glanced quickly around the room, catching the grand piano and floor-to-ceiling windows and the fireplace that could have easily contained me, standing up. I supposed there was more than one way to define "high and dry."

"We were high school sweethearts," Jill continued and I got the distinct impression she was launching into a story that was well worn. "He was captain of the football team, I was lead cheerleader." She smiled ruefully. "He loved my legs and I loved his hair. He still has great hair, doesn't he?" She seemed genuinely curious.

I nodded. "Awesome hair."

She looked pleased, as if she had something to do with Beau's coif. "Well, it's probably not the best idea to get married because of legs and hair, but I suppose people have done it for less." She smiled a bit, and seemed to be remembering, though it could have been the drink taking effect. "We did good, actually. He worked too hard and I was hacked off at him for years when he didn't help enough with the kids. He'd get mad when I'd stay out too late with the girls. You know. All the normal stuff." She shrugged. "But nothing too terrible."

I waited while she got up to refresh her drink.

"You sure you don't want anything?" she asked over a bony shoulder.

One of the sequins on the "tasty" motif caught sunlight and I squinted. I was squinting because of a brilliant butt. This morning could not have gotten any weirder.

"I'm fine, thanks," I said and waited as she resettled herself on the couch, tucking her feet under her. "So what went wrong?"

She gathered her long frosted blonde hair with her free hand and let it fall down one shoulder. "It started falling apart during Piper's senior year. Piper is our youngest. Jack's our oldest. They are both out of college now. Jack is an investment banker in Manhattan and Piper lives in Los Angeles and waits tables when she's not auditioning. She's an actress." Pride shone in Jill's eyes and softened what had been there during the rest of our conversation.

"I have a daughter too. Her name is Nora." I smiled. "She is also an actress and in constant state of auditioning. I should teach her to wait tables, at least earn her keep."

Jill's smile seemed sad. "How old is she?"

"Five," I said. "Going on twenty."

Jill nodded knowingly. "Those are great years. I miss them being small enough to pick them up and force kisses on them. New York and Dublin are too far away for kisses." She stared in her drink, then took a dainty sip. "Of course, they both left as soon as they could to escape all the tension around here. And here's the weird part." She pointed at me with her index finger, the rest of her fingers curled around her glass. Her face was a little flushed. "We were fine during the bankruptcy. Honest to God. Totally fine. It was afterwards that it got bad."

"Bankruptcy?" I searched my memories of conversations with Willow and Beau and couldn't remember anything about bankruptcy.

"Oh, didn't you know?" Jill said, sarcasm dripping. "Beau Vaughn, the man who could do no wrong, the one who could make money in his sleep, declared professional bankruptcy. It was the talk of the town, I'll give you that." She shook her head. "All the people who had invested in his company and lost all their money. People who had been our friends for years and all of a sudden wouldn't invite us to dinner and wouldn't even talk to me when we ran into each other on the sidewalk. They'd cross to the other side and I'm not even kidding. He lost it all." She narrowed her eyes. "Doesn't your friend want to know all this? Hey," she said suddenly, looking around the room, "where *is* your friend? Doesn't she want to hear all this herself?" Jill's words were starting to slur together a bit.

"I'll be sure to tell her," I said hurriedly. I needed to hear the rest of this story and by the pliable look on Jill's sculpted face I knew my minutes were numbered before Jill either fell asleep or pulled out the karaoke machine and revved up some Bon Jovi. "I'm sorry if this too personal but how are you still living in this house if Beau lost it all? I guess I haven't asked you about your work. You must have a fantastic job?"

She barked out a laugh. "I've never worked a day in my life," she said, and I couldn't tell from her tone if she was proud or angry. "Beau made all the money and Beau lost all the money. All I could do was watch. And support." She took awhile but did, in fact, focus her gaze on my eyes. "I supported him. When no one else supported him. When everyone else said he was a goner. I was still there. Not that it made any difference." She tossed back the rest of her drink with an ease that made me sure these two installments had followed Bloody Marys, maybe a mimosa or two, before I'd even gotten to her front door. I resisted the urge to take the empty glass and tuck her into bed with a jug of water and a bottle of aspirin.

"We didn't know how to talk anymore by the time it was all over. It was almost as if the struggle of the bankruptcy had taken over and once all that was resolved and we were able to move on, we couldn't." She shut her eyes. "We'd been faking it for a long time. Saying you forgive someone and actually forgiving them are two completely different things."

I watched her face and felt an overwhelming sadness. Her story, Beau's story, was sad and lonely and isolating. Everything I didn't want for Willow. She'd had enough of all those things dealing with Michael's illness and death. I cleared my throat and was about to say good-bye when Jill's eyelids flew open. She fixed her stare on me, and if I hadn't known any better, I'd have thought she was completely sober.

"You tell your friend Beau Vaughn is not who he says he is.

Has he taken her to Guido's? Has she met Paulo the wonder chef? I'm the one who introduced Beau to Paulo, by the way." She stabbed her finger into the air to emphasize her point. "Has she met him?"

I nodded, my throat dry.

She smiled in a way that did not make her look any prettier. "Of course he has. She is one in a long, long line of women who have been to that restaurant with him. And she might be the first one who's gotten a marriage proposal, but she won't be the last to have her heart broken by Beau." Jill's words caught at the end and her eyes filled. The tears didn't change the angry expression on her face. "Your friend is a fool if she marries him. I sure was." She shook her head slowly back and forth, back and forth for so long that I didn't know if she remembered I was there.

Finally, into the silence I spoke. "Thank you for meeting with me."

She said nothing, just closed her eyes. "I need a drink," she said, eyes still closed. "You want anything?"

I shook my head but she wasn't really looking for me to answer.

"I can find my way out," I said as she walked carefully to the cocktail cart.

When I found the front door, I stepped through and shuddered at the hollow sound it made when I pulled it shut behind me.

19

Marlys, the Copper Creek librarian, brought me a second cup of tea, which I gathered was an egregious illegal act considering how she presented it to me with great ceremony and then adjusted a mini-partition of books to hide it from the hypothetical other patrons. No one else was actually using the reference room at the Copper Creek Library, but one couldn't be too careful.

"Let me know if you need anything else," Marlys whispered. Her teased auburn hair quivered in front as she patted my shoulder. "Anything at all." She raised her voice to something of a growl. "Take him down."

I winced into my hot tea as she padded back to the circulation desk in her loafers. Marlys had a bone to pick and I had done her the favor of making the first incision. After leaving Jill's house, I'd looked at the clock and had seen that I didn't need to be back in Springdale for two hours, so when I spotted the sign for the library, I'd acted on impulse and swerved into the nearly empty parking lot. Marlys had greeted me from her post at the front desk, and when I explained I wanted to do some research on a former resident of Copper Creek, she had been most accommodating. There was the tea, of course, but there was also a colorful litany on the demerits of Beau Vaughn. Marlys knew Beau, or rather, Marlys knew Beau's wake of destruction. Marlys had a sister, Palmyra, and Palmyra's bank account had been ransacked after Beau's poor investments on her behalf. Oh, did I get an earful. Just because Marlys was fond of ankle-length skirts and sweater sets did not mean that Marlys didn't have some colorful language under her braided belt when it came to Beau Vaughn. Poor Palmyra had to change her retirement plans. Poor Palmyra had to sell her late husband's Harley Davidson motorcycle. Poor Palmyra kept her house but had to cancel plans for a kitchen remodel.

Poor Palmyra was the reason I was getting multiple cups of tea and a waived photocopier fee.

I was listening to Marlys talk about her cavapoo puppy, Leonard, as she refilled the paper trays within the bowels of the copier when I glanced at the clock on the wall and felt my stomach drop.

"Oh, no!" I yelped, already dashing back to my spot at the worktable. I pawed at the papers I'd accumulated and stuffed them into my purse, then slung the purse over my shoulder and yanked my coat off the back of the chair.

"Is everything all right?" Marlys whispered loudly from the copier across the room.

"I'm late for a very important appointment," I whispered back, feeling ridiculous as Marlys and I were the only ones in the room. "Thank you for all your help, Marlys," I whispered as I backed out of the reference section and toward the front door. "For all your input. And for the tea," I added, pointing to the hot cup still on the table.

"My pleasure," she said and did some sort of salute with a raised fist. What kind of man was Beau Vaughn, I mused as I fumbled for my car keys, that such different women, one in a tight-fitting jumpsuit and one wearing leather loafers and rosewater perfume, both go into a militant mode when his name comes up in conversation? I threw the gearshift in reverse and booked it to the highway, heading out of town and toward trouble.

✦ ✦ ✦

"I'm so sorry," I said, breathless, into my cell phone. Having proven once again that, despite my wishful thinking and lead foot, the Civic was not capable of traveling faster than the speed of light, I was giving in and calling Jake to tell him I was going to be late. Very late.

"A half hour?" Jake said, clearly upset. "The social worker is going to be here any second. Where are you in Springdale that it will take you a half hour to get home?"

"I'm not in Springdale," I said, wincing with the words. "I'm on my way back from Copper Creek. I was doing some research and lost track of time."

I could practically hear the wheels clicking as Jake tried to piece together what I was saying. "You were doing research in Copper Creek. Research on what?" He paused and then said, softening a bit, "On adoption?"

Crap. "No," I said slowly. "On, um, Beau Vaughn. He lived there for a long time, turns out. And it's really good I went, Jake. I talked with this woman—"

"Don't," he said, a razor-sharp edge in his voice. "I don't want to know, Heidi. And I don't want to talk about it right now because the social worker is pulling into our driveway and I can't be screaming at my absent wife on the phone when she walks in."

I sucked in my breath, wounded by his words but knowing the wounds were entirely my own fault. "I'll be there as soon as I can. I'm so sorry."

"Pretend we have a great marriage when you get here, okay? Let's just get through this." He hung up.

I pushed down harder on the gas.

✦ ✦ ✦

I stood, heart racing and out-of-breath, on my front porch. I held my hand on the front door a second, gathering myself to audition in my own house. Just be yourself, I thought, and then discarded that stupid idea. Being myself had gotten me a half hour late and into a fight with my husband.

I pushed open the door and was met with silence. Letting the door latch quietly behind me, I slipped off my shoes and listened, finally hearing Jake clear his throat in the dining room. I rounded the corner into the room and Nora threw down the crayon she was using and ran to me. I smiled hopefully over her head as I hugged her. Jake's facial expression was neutral. The woman sitting next to him smiled back, which I took as encouragement, small as it was.

"Mommy!" Nora said into my coat and then pulled back. She turned to the woman at the table and brandished her arm like a used car salesman. "Mrs. Marek, this is my mom. Mom, this is Mrs. Marek. She's watching us to see if a baby is safe here."

I reached over the table to shake Mrs. Marek's hand. "Welcome," I said. "I'm so very sorry I'm late."

Mrs. Marek looked pleasant but also a little like she'd had experience in the military. Her posture was impeccable and I had the distinct impression she had ironed and starched the white camisole under her button-down. "I've had the chance to chat with Nora and Jake, so not all is lost."

Nora looked at Mrs. Marek and used her explaining voice. "This is the mom that used to help in my class at school before Gus Hill chopped off his finger. Now she staples stuff for my teacher but not in our classroom."

Oh, dear Lord, have mercy, I prayed. I glanced at Jake, who was giving me absolutely nothing with his blank stare and vaguely pleasant expression.

"Wow," I said, feeling my mouth go dry. "You heard that story?"

Mrs. Marek nodded, and I thought I saw a hint of mischief in her eyes. "We sure did. Nora has been quite the conversationalist."

"Great," I said through my teeth. "That's really great."

Mrs. Marek sat straighter in her chair, a feat I had not thought possible, and she pushed her reading glasses further up her nose. "I have your home study application here, so I know all the basics. Ages, marriage date, health histories, and so on. I've asked Jake a few questions about his parenting philosophy, but why don't you tell me a bit about your own views on parenting, Heidi. For example, how do you approach discipline?"

"Discipline," I repeated, sounding like I was at a spelling bee and about to ask for the language of origin. I folded my hands on the dining room table I'd polished just that morning and tried to relax. "Well, Nora has a lot of spunk and sometimes the spunk needs to be redirected. Or corrected." I watched as Nora started her coloring again. "I've found that time-outs are pretty effective because Nora is social and doesn't like to be taken away from the fun."

Mrs. Marek turned to Nora. "What do you think about

time-outs, Nora?"

Nora pulled a face. "They are disgusting and horrible." She tilted her head in thought. "But sometimes I forget I'm in time-out and I play with my dolls, which is much better. And," she pointed her crayon at Mrs. Marek's nose, "time-outs are way, way better than yelling."

Mrs. Marek started scribbling on the paper in front of her.

"Nora," I began, but she ignored me.

"Dad's yells are the worst," Nora said, happily coloring Rapunzel's hair Day-Glo yellow. "I'm *terrified* of those. Mom's yells aren't so bad, but she does get a really scary, red face when she does them. Right, Mom?"

Mrs. Marek continued to write. I looked at Silent Jake, pleading silently with him to stop the madness.

"We do raise our voices but sparingly," Jake said, sounding far more confident than I felt.

"Is that okay?" I said and immediately regretted the needy tone in my voice. "I mean, that's okay, right? We'll hardly ever yell at a baby. Never, actually. We would never, ever yell at a baby. Not until she or he was at least two. And then she'd be naughty and trying to test every rule in the book, which means our yelling would probably not even soak in. So it shouldn't count." Oh. Good. Heavenly. Days. Shut up, woman.

Ms. Marek nodded curtly. "My role is simply to observe and listen, not to pass judgment on your decisions. If those decisions interfere with what I believe would be best for an adopted child, then I intervene."

Man, this lady was good. I felt like I was listening to a political debate. Answers that weren't answers at all. I swallowed hard and widened my eyes at Jake, willing him to look up from his folded hands. He did not.

"Tell me, Jake, why you have decided to pursue adoption." Mrs. Marek held her pen poised above a blank space on her form.

Jake's face relaxed. "The most obvious answer is that we have struggled unsuccessfully with infertility for a long time, and we would love to add another child to our home. But for me it's more than that." Jake paused and looked at Nora, who was lining up the crayons in rainbow order. "I know it might sound bizarre, but I feel this in my spirit, way down deep. I know I'm supposed to be a dad for a child who needs a dad. I've prayed about this for a very long time. Sometimes I even tried to will it away. Adoption is not convenient. It's expensive. It's emotionally taxing. And that's just the part leading up to the birth."

Mrs. Marek nodded, waiting.

Jake shrugged. "But I know this pull in my spirit won't go away. And I know I'm supposed to keep pushing doors open until I meet the child who will become a part of our family. I can't wait." Jake's voice broke a little during the last sentence, and Mrs. Marek seemed to be studying his face. Apparently satisfied, she returned her gaze to her paper and resumed writing.

I looked down at the hands I clenched in my lap. Jake's answer was beautiful and heart-deep and I wished I would have heard it first when we were alone together, sitting on our front porch as the sun went down and Nora was tucked into bed. I bit my bottom lip, feeling a shock of resentment pulse through me. I wanted him to say those things to me, not to Mrs. Marek. I also wanted to have something in my own answer that sounded like *that*.

Mrs. Marek lifted her head from the form. "Heidi? Tell me about why you have decided to adopt a child."

I tried clearing my throat but my voice still sounded scratchy and timid when I responded. "I want a baby. And I don't think I can have any more babies on my own. So adoption seems like our only choice."

"So you don't feel the same kind of calling or pull that Jake does?" Mrs. Marek's tone was impassive, as if she hadn't just asked a question that could rip a girl's heart in two.

"That's not what I mean," I said, looking at Jake, who was furrowing his brow as he listened to me stumble. "I do. I mean, I do want a baby and have wanted one for years. Adoption is just a lot to take in, so I'm still processing it all. But I do feel called to have another child. I do. Very much." I felt my shoulders slump even as I spoke. Mrs. Marek had written throughout my mangled answer. I didn't even want to know how she was assessing my readiness in comparison to Jake's.

"Well, *I* sure want a baby," Nora said, startling me into remembering she was sitting there and was hearing every word. "I'm going to be a really good big sister. I'm going to share my Barbies and my clothes and my Legos but only the big ones because otherwise she'll choke." She raised her eyebrows at Mrs. Marek to let that last tidbit sink in. "I'm very safe for babies. But the baby can't play with my American Girl doll or I'll have to hit the baby pretty hard."

"Nora!" I said sternly.

"Okay, fine," she relented. "But I *will* bite her."

"Norie, we don't bite people when they don't do what we want," I said in my best conciliatory tone that could also indicate to my daughter that she was on thin ice.

"Yes, we do," she said cheerily. "Remember when I was little and I bit people and you said I couldn't do that anymore but I didn't stop? And then I bit you? So you bit my arm. Remember, Mom? That was pretty funny."

Jake's head was now in his hands.

"I did bite you on your arm," I said, my voice at an unnaturally high pitch. "Not too hard and just once. I didn't think you were understanding that biting hurt, so I thought I should show you." Mrs. Marek just kept writing with that infernal pen of hers while I was starting to feel sweat trickle down my neck. The woman was merciless. "You did learn your lesson. You never bit anyone again," I finished meekly, fully aware that Nora already knew the moral of this family legend and that my retelling of it was for Mrs. Marek's benefit alone.

"I didn't even bleed very much," Nora said to start me daydreaming about other legal avenues of corporal punishment. "Not like Gus Hill."

Mrs. Marek stayed at our house for another two interminable hours. The highlights (or lowlights), in order of occurrence:

1. A brief but convicting lecture on home safety and how we were miserable failures. Jake sat down to his iPad in Mrs. Marek's presence and ordered a fire extinguisher, two extra smoke detectors, three carbon monoxide detectors, and a ridiculous, bulky fire escape ladder to be stored in Nora's room alongside her Barbie house and the pinch-worthy American Girl doll. When Jake suggested we stop cooking with a gas stove and instead consider going all microwave, all the time, I threw him a look that made the words wither in his mouth. Score one and only one for the missus.

2. During a discussion of extended family relationships, Nora went on at length about my Uncle Bill, who favored showing up to family gatherings completely plowed. Nora loved Uncle Bill because the more inebriated he became, the more wrinkled dollar bills he pushed

into Nora's waiting palm. So Mrs. Marek got an earful about substance abuse *and* my daughter's extortion tendencies. The pen scribbled on.

3. Nora threw open the medicine chest in our bathroom in search of her favorite ladybug toothbrush and front and center, eye-level with Mrs. Marek, was a tube of jock itch cream and a bottle of personal lubricant. When Jake slammed shut the cabinet, we were faced with three reddening faces in the mirror and a whining Nora who was sure she'd seen the ladybug toothbrush right before Jake shut the door.

By the time we eased the front door closed behind Mrs. Marek, I was spent. Jake and I walked numbly to the family room and I let myself drop heavily onto the couch. Jake took an armchair and groaned as he let his head drop back.

"Brutal," he said, staring at the ceiling.

I moaned a little to express agreement.

"That was so fun!" Nora said. She plopped down onto the space beside me. "We should have Mrs. Marek over again."

"No," I groaned. "We shouldn't. Never, ever, ever."

"Mom!" Nora said, shock on her face. "That's not polite at all. Mrs. Marek was supernice. She used whole body listening every time she asked me a question. And she asked a *bazillion* questions."

"At least a bazillion," Jake said from his prone state on the chair.

"Do you think we passed?" I said. I closed my eyes so I wouldn't have to see the disappointment on Jake's face.

He waited a long time before answering. "I don't know," he finally said. "I'm not sure we should."

I sat up a bit and looked at my husband. For the first time in hours, he met my gaze.

"Heidi, I keep hearing you say yes with your mouth but I still feel like I'm the one pulling us along here. We can't do adoption like this." He passed his hand over his face, weariness showing in the slump of his shoulders. "We can't keep going like this. You go on researching road trips without telling me, you blow off our home visit—"

"I didn't blow it off," I began but stopped when Jake held up his hand.

"Don't. No more excuses."

I felt Nora become still beside me. She could feel the shift in the room and must have instinctively known she needed to be quiet and let Jake speak. I certainly did.

"We have to be together in this or not at all. You have to decide if you want to adopt or not. No more riding the current, going along with it and letting me make all the decisions. I did not marry a robot, and I can't stand spineless women. I did not marry a spineless woman."

I suspected there was a compliment in there somewhere but my heart was so heavy, I didn't even absorb it.

"You need to figure out what you want," Jake said. He stood and shoved his hands in his pockets. "I'm tired of trying to figure it out for you."

He walked over to Nora and picked her up. "Let's go pick up some pizza, squirt," he said. "You hungry?"

"Yep," she said. She kept her eyes on me, her chin nestled over Jake's shoulder as he carried her to the front door. I smiled shakily at her.

"We'll get your favorite kind, Mom," she said. "No olives."

"Thanks, kiddo," I said. I watched them go, hearing the

screen door click shut and Jake's footsteps on the porch floor. The hollowness in my gut, I knew, would not be filled after dinner, no matter if they got my favorite or not.

20

The following morning was chilly all around. Jake was courteous as he got ready for work, moving out of the way so I could be the first to the coffee pot, apologizing for reaching for the fridge door just as I did. I hated it. Courtesy was one teeny step up from a shouting match, in my opinion, maybe even a step below. At least during a shouting match we could be less careful with each other.

And then, when Nora and I stepped onto the porch to begin our trek to school, we squealed in unison.

"It's freezing!" Nora said, already shivering within her jacket. The bright sunshine was a ruse because we were definitely experiencing our first cold snap. I wheeled her around and we went back into the house. From the top shelf of the hall closet, I tugged down baskets of winter gear: hats, gloves, scarves, the errant mitten, Jake's balaclava used for snowblowing. Nora rummaged within the baskets to assemble her accessories while I flipped through the hangers to locate our warm winter coats, neglected since spring.

"We're going to be late!" Nora called, nose deep within a pile of hats. "I hate being late!"

"We'll be fine," I snapped, already fully on my way to cranky at a very early hour. "Just go fast."

"I'm trying," she said, and I could hear the panic and imminent tears in her voice.

I tossed over her green and white polka dot jacket. "Here. Winter coat," I said while shrugging into my own down jacket. "Let's shake what our mamas gave us."

"I can't," Nora wailed, her limbs flailing as she tried to find the armholes. "I can't do it!"

"Oh, for the love of Pete," I muttered as I stepped over a pile of outerwear to get to her. I helped get her coat zipped, pushed a stocking hat down over her eyebrows, and then I helped her with mittens, knowing only a fool would attempt gloves in such a fragile moment.

"These don't match my coat," Nora said, her bottom lip trembling.

"They look fine," I snapped and roughly coerced the second mitten onto Nora's hand. "Let's go."

We walked quickly, me shouldering Nora's backpack, Nora whimpering every now and then to slow down. I was racking up gold seals for motherhood with each step.

When we reached the front doors of the school, one of the last families to trickle onto school grounds, I pulled Nora into a quick hug.

"The last bell hasn't rung yet," I said, words tumbling. "Hurry and you'll make it to your desk in time." I kissed her on her cheek.

"'Bye, Mom," Nora said, face downcast. I felt a pang of guilt as she scurried away, her backpack so big on her back, it bounced on the backs of her knees as she walked.

Not a great start to a day, I thought, shoving my gloved hands into my pockets and starting back home. My nose was a pink icicle by the time I took the porch stairs two at a time and unlocked the front door. A rush of warm air greeted me and I stood in my hat and gloves a moment to thaw. From within my coat, my phone sounded a muffled ring. I retrieved it, saw it was Annie calling, and declined the call for the fourth time in about as many days. I fired off a quick text to delay actual conversation, an art I was perfecting.

"Can't talk," I typed. "Just getting Nora to school," I wrote, a not-actual lie as this was true, though Nora was no longer within my line of sight. "I'll try touching base later! Love you!" I sent the message, knowing I would not be touching base any time that day. Or the next day. Or the next, until I could muster some courage to listen to Annie talk about her pregnancy symptoms and her latest trip to BabyGap and the way James had taken to singing to the baby every night before bed. Our last ten conversations had touched on all these things and by the end of the last one, I felt bile rising in my throat. I'd reasoned with myself all the way through and for hours afterward, reminding myself that God asked me to rejoice with those who rejoiced and that it was my responsibility as Annie's friend to be excited with her as she walked through her pregnancy.

All that pep talking had produced very little in the way of acceptance, but I had gotten very good at biding time with avoidance texts.

I opened the hall closet and turned on the light. Unzipping my coat, I reached for an empty hanger and stopped. On the top shelf, against the wall, I glimpsed the manila folder I'd stashed there in a hurry when I flew in the door the night before. I'd been in a rush to hang up my coat and get to the home study conversation occurring in the dining room. On the way, I'd tucked the papers from my Copper Creek visit out of sight in the closet. I reached up now and pulled the file away from its hiding place. My fingers, still cold from my walk, paged through the sheets of paper, reading snippets of my notes, seeing the photos of Beau on the printouts of newspaper articles. I felt the familiar gnawing settle in my gut and I reached for my phone. Enough was enough. It was time to spill what I knew to Willow before she took one more step toward a walk down the aisle to Beau.

She answered on the second ring. "Heidi!" she said, joy filling her voice. "I'm so glad to hear from you!"

"Hi," I said, frowning to think of how very *not* glad she might be to hear what I had to say. "Hey, do you have a few minutes this morning? Can you meet for coffee?"

"Absolutely," she said, and I knew she didn't even check her calendar. Willow was not a calendar-checking friend. She was a forget-the-calendar-let's-meet-for-coffee friend. "Sophie can cover the counter. Do you want to swing by here around ten? Thing should be pretty quiet by then."

"Perfect," I said before I could lose my nerve. "See you soon." I hung up and took a deep breath, let it out slowly. It was time for the big reveal.

✦   ✦   ✦

Willow's café was housed in a former church. The sanctuary rose upward into waves of soaring Gothic arches, offering perfect light and airiness for the small art gallery it hosted. I made my way through where pews used to line the rows of St. Peter's Episcopal. Weaving through the work of five or six artist groupings, I glanced at ceramics, acrylics, mixed media, and a beautiful, gutsy line of watercolors. At the far end of the room, I reached the narrow, creaking staircase that led to the old choir loft and Willow's little café. She was leaning against the mosaic counter that framed the bottom of a soaring, circular stained glass window. She waved to me when she saw me take an empty table against the railing. I waited for her to join me, forcing my eyes to focus on the beams of light pouring into the sanctuary below instead of thinking about the pool of dread in my stomach.

"Gorgeous, right?" Willow said as she took the seat opposite mine and followed my gaze. "The light in this room shifts throughout the day and honestly, it's my very favorite show to watch. Beats *The Bachelorette*." She laughed and I smiled, knowing well the sermon that could ensue at any moment when Willow started in on the way reality television objectified women. For once, I wished she would launch into a rant and buy me a little time.

"It will be the perfect spot for the wedding," she said, eyes soft. "We'll have a small job relocating all the artwork within the building, but it will be worth it." She turned to me. "Heidi it is so, so good to see you," Willow said and reached over to take both of my hands. I watched the flecks in her green eyes pick up the light in the room and flash deep gold. "I've missed you. We've both been so busy."

I nodded. "I've missed you too." I cleared my throat. "How's Beau?" *Please say you broke up yesterday and that I won't have to tell you what a cad he is because you already know.*

Willow sighed a blissful sigh. "Beau is wonderful. Kind, thoughtful, funny, smart. Last night he took me to a poetry reading in Minneapolis and then out to an Ecuadorian restaurant." She closed her eyes, remembering. "I'll never see sweet fried plantains in the same way."

I bit my lower lip. "You really love him."

She opened her eyes and grinned. "I really do. He takes me

on adventures and I love going where he takes me." She paused, thoughtful. "Michael was a total gift from God. He understood me, even as a teenager, and we grew together. We loved each other so deeply, I thought I wouldn't ever feel that way about anyone again. And I was right, in a way. I don't feel the same for Beau because Beau is a different person. But I do love him. Fiercely. Ferociously. In a way that will grow and deepen, just like it did with Michael." Her eyes were shining, and the look on her face made my throat constrict.

I swallowed. "I'm sorry I couldn't join you for the dress shopping."

She waved away my apology with one hand. "No biggie. I didn't find anything anyway. Lots of billowy chiffon in those stores. Not exactly my style. I'm going to try some shops in Minneapolis in a couple weekends. Hey!" She clasped her hands, excited. "Maybe you can come! We could make a day of it. Shops, bookstores, good food. Jake could take Nora for the day, right?"

I cleared my throat. *Do it. Now.* "Willow," I said, my voice suddenly shaky, "we need to talk."

Willow let her hands fall to her lap. Her brow furrowed. "Okay. Let's talk."

"It's about Beau," I began. "He's not who he says he is."

Willow widened her eyes. "What do you mean?"

"I've been doing some checking into some of the things he says about himself," I said, taking my time and trying to organize my thoughts. "And I think he's been lying. To you, to me, to everyone."

Willow became very still. "Go on."

"All right," I said, letting out a long breath. "I'll start from the beginning. First, Beau keeps talking about how Springdale is so cute, so quaint, so small town. Like he's never been to a small town before and certainly not lived in one, at least not other than college and a brief stint somewhere else. Right?"

Willow said nothing.

"Well, that's a lie. Beau lived very close to here for over twenty years. Willow, Beau lived in Copper Creek. As in forty-minutes-away Copper Creek."

She narrowed her eyes. "Copper Creek?" A light went on. "Wait. Is that where you were driving yesterday when I called you about the dress?"

"Yes," I said, reaching for my purse under the table. I pulled out the manila folder. "I went there to check into some things."

"You went to Copper Creek," Willow said, starting to repeat herself. First signs of shock. "Yesterday. You drove there and couldn't meet me to look at dresses because you were going to Copper Creek to check into Beau's past."

I nodded and started flipping through my notes. "It was no problem. I knew you were so trusting of people, you would never do any Internet research on Beau, much less go nose around his home town. I didn't mind taking the trip at all." I pulled out the photocopies of news articles and held them to my chest, waiting to give Willow the rest of the story before the hard evidence.

"Willow, Beau left a wake behind him when he moved away from Copper Creek. He filed bankruptcy after failed invest-ments, and many people in the town lost nearly everything because of his poor choices. I met one of them, well, the sister of one of his victims, and she is still angry about the way Beau destroyed her sister's bank account."

Willow's jaw had set in a hard line. Second stage: anger. "Who was this woman?"

"She works in the library. She helped me find these." I

pushed the papers to her side of the table. "These articles were all written during the time of the bankruptcy filings, the arbitration, all that. And I'm very concerned about all this, not only because he hasn't been forthright about it but because," I paused, took a deep breath. "Because I think Beau might be doing the same thing again."

"Filing for bankruptcy?"

I shook my head. "No. I think he might be preying on women to get them to invest in his company. A company that has a beautiful but completely unclear website. I spent some time looking at it but still have no idea what Beau does."

"I see," Willow said, her lips drawn in a straight line. "You are concerned about me being taken advantage of and about Beau's sketchy job."

"Yes," I said, relieved she was getting to the crux of the matter. "I just don't want you to be the next in a long line. I don't want you to end up like Jill."

Something hard flickered in Willow's eyes when I said Jill's name. "You mean Jill, Beau's ex-wife."

I nodded, swallowed hard. "I met her too. In fact, she's the one who led me to Copper Creek. We met on Facebook." I started talking faster when I saw Willow shake her head. "I know, it's a little odd, and I thought about telling you, but I know how you hate social media and how you would never try to contact Jill yourself. I felt I needed to ask her some questions and that I owed you that as your friend."

"It was your duty," Willow said, and I thought I heard some sharpness in her voice, but I didn't blame her. If she'd seen what I saw, the sharpness wouldn't even be that masked.

"She's very angry," I said. "After all of Beau's financial troubles, she thought he would stick around. I mean, I'm sure she's not perfect, but surely he owed her enough to stay after all they went through together."

"What did you think of the house?" Willow asked.

I made a face. "Very showy. Nothing like you at all."

She nodded. "The sculpture in the foyer is a knockoff."

I took a sharp intake of breath. "Wait. You've been to the house?"

She raised an eyebrow. "Twice, actually. When we first started dating, Piper and Jack were home at the same time and we went over so Beau could see them and introduce me to them. And most recently, we were there last week to deliver some home insurance documents Beau found when cleaning out his apartment to get ready to move after the wedding."

"So you've met Jill?" I swallowed hard. "She didn't mention that. In fact, she acted like she didn't know about you and Beau."

Willow nodded slowly. "Jill has a history of telling only the parts of stories that interest her, which may or may not be the truthful parts." Willow sat up straight in her chair. "Did she mention that she has a long history of having affairs, the first one starting two months after their honeymoon?"

I shook my head. I didn't like the edge in Willow's voice.

"Did she mention that Beau has paid for and supported her through not four but five—five!—stints in alcoholic rehab? Even paying for one stay *after* their divorce?"

I shook my head again, my stomach roiling.

"And did she say that Piper and Jack have all but cut ties with their mother because of her pathological lying tendencies and that the only relationship that has been salvaged remains because Beau has begged them to stay in touch? Because even though Jill is horribly damaged and bitter and broken, she is still their mother? Did she say any of that as she sat in the enormous house Beau purchased with his hard work while he lives in a studio apartment with a window air conditioning unit?" By the time Willow finished speaking, her voice was raised. Sophie looked up from cleaning the espresso machine across the room, a question mark in her expression.

"Willow," I said softly, "I didn't know any of that."

"Of course you didn't!" She threw up her hands. "You couldn't have known any of that because you never asked me. You asked *Jill.*" She leaned across the table to me. "Jill, who was such a hot mess after the divorce, Beau completely shifted his business focus to helping women cope with the collateral damage after a divorce so their children didn't suffer like the Vaughn kids did. *That* Jill." She lifted her hands, struggling to get the words out fast enough. "Heidi, what were you thinking? Going all Nancy Drew instead of just asking me, your friend who has seen you through marital strife, child-rearing, faith crises, infertility?"

I shook my head quickly, willing away what she was saying and clinging to my own resolve. "I couldn't ask you. You're blinded by love. And you would never Google search."

"Oh, so that's it?" She spat the words. "I'm old and stupid and I don't know how to work a computer? Well, you know what, Heidi? I can see this will come as a surprise to you, but Beau and I have already talked about all this." She narrowed her eyes. "Back in the olden days we didn't depend on Facebook to get to know someone. Back then we used our brains and our hearts and we listened and talked and spent time with someone to get to know them. Which is why this hurts so much. I know you. And you know me. And that didn't count for anything when you set off in your car to meet with Jill and then lie to me about what you were doing."

Willow's chest was heaving and she was staring at my face. I felt like I was about to be sick, but I couldn't quite agree with what Willow was saying. She was angry, yes, and I could understand that, but she still didn't know the full story. I thought of BVaughn's profile, his request to connect, and of the e-mail I'd received just that morning, asking to meet me.

"Willow, there's more," I began, but she stopped me with her hand. Light flashed briefly, picking up the sparkle in her engagement ring.

"No," she said. "I've heard more than enough. You've done enough. I'm going to do with you what I used to do with Michael and the boys when we would have an argument. I'm going to say what I used to say to them, which is, 'I can't believe you just said that. I'm hurt and reeling and I need some time before we talk about this again.'" She stood up, eyes still flashing. "I love you, Heidi, and that won't change. But you have hurt me. I know you are aching for a baby and that the last couple of years have been brutal. You're feeling a bit rudderless. I know that."

I dug shaking fingers into my palms, not speaking.

"But you've done this all wrong. I can't function in a friendship that entertains dishonesty. Can't do it." She waved halfheartedly and started backing away. "You need to go."

I watched her turn her back to me and walk to Sophie, who still wore a question mark on her face. Gathering my things, I stood, numb. And I put one foot in front of the other to obey my friend. Without another word, I left.

21

The heavy doors of St. Peter's fell shut behind me with a dull thud that echoed in the chilly air. A gust of wind sent brittle leaves shivering in the branches above me, and I stood on the limestone steps of the church, letting Willow's words and the hurt look in her eyes settle into my thoughts. She just didn't understand. She didn't *want* to understand. That was the problem. She wasn't willing to look at the big picture, and it was easiest to take it out on me. I wasn't the first messenger to be killed because of the bad news she brought.

I started down the steps, hands buried deep in the pockets of my coat. My head was down and I was lost in my own world, so I didn't see Annie and James until they were right in front of me. I looked up, vaguely aware Annie's voice had been calling my name for a while.

"Oh. Hi," I said, still distracted but trying to summon some sort of social grace to have a quick conversation and then reach my car, which was parked just behind the couple. "I didn't see you there."

James laughed in a low, musical bass. "We noticed. You looked like you were far away in your own thoughts, Heidi Elliott."

I nodded, wanting to get to back to those thoughts as soon as possible. "What are you two up to?" I glanced at their clothes. "Not running, I see. You're too spiffy for that. And no one's sweating."

Annie smiled. "Good deductive reasoning, detective." Her hair swung around her shoulders when she laughed. How was it possible that some women became more beautiful and radiant when pregnant while the rest of us merely became living, daily examples of the "before" photo? "We just finished our registry at Sweet Pea." She looked up at James, eyes shining. "It was so much fun, I want to go back and do it all again, right now."

James rolled his eyes. "Two hundred fifty dollars for a diaper bag? Heidi, this woman needs to be restrained for her own health and the health of our child. No infant needs denim, in any form. And yet my wife just registered for Hudson jeans. *Designer jeans.* For a human that will top out at eight, nine pounds at the most. I am a grown man, and *I* don't have Hudson jeans."

Annie shrugged. "You're welcome to get some. They do wonders for your butt."

James let out a sharp laugh. "So now we're trying to improve on diaper butt? That's why you put jeans on the list?"

I couldn't do it any more. "You'll never use them. Total waste of money. Babies hate rigid fabrics like that. You'll stuff him or her into them one time and then regret it because he or she will poop all the way up the back and you'll have to use precious nap time Googling how to get poop out of designer denim when you really should be icing your swollen nipples or showering for the first time in days or just crying. Sobbing uncontrollably takes a surprising amount of time."

I stopped, noting the look of shock and horror on both of their faces. Annie opened her mouth and then closed it again.

"Sorry," I mumbled. "I probably said too much."

"Probably," James said, his face somber.

"I'll go." I said, stepping around them and giving wide berth, afraid if I got any closer to Annie's belly, I'd inflict more collateral damage. "I'll call you later, Annie."

"Really?" she said, and I heard the sarcasm in her voice. "Because that hasn't been happening much lately," she called after me. I waved behind me, not trusting myself for another response. Heidi the Witty was fresh out of faking it today, and I thought it best to just get in my car and get out of there. I didn't look up as I put my car in reverse and drove, my heart racing.

I was losing my mind. And my patience. And any sort of control over my tongue.

What is wrong with me? I thought as I pulled to a stop at a red light in the middle of downtown. My phone vibrated from within my purse and I started digging to locate it. Maybe it was Willow, calling to patch things up, saying she'd had some time to think and wanted to hear what else I had to say. The phone stopped vibrating and I could feel my shoulders deflate, knowing it wasn't a call but an incoming e-mail. The light was still red so I swiped into my e-mail, assuming it was my coupon for Bed Bath & Beyond because it was always my coupon for Bed Bath & Beyond. My heart skipped when I saw the sender: BVaughn.

To: LibrarianLizzie456@gmail.com

From: BV4real!@hotmail.com

Hey, Lizzie. Let's be spontaneous. Life is too short, right?

I'm coming up on a very big decision, life-altering stuff. And I want to meet you before I make the jump. Can you meet this afternoon? Like right now? I'm typing fast and sending quickly, before I can talk myself back into a more reasonable position.

Say yes.

Actually, don't say anything. Just come. Meet me at the coffee shop on the corner of Broad and Jackson in an hour. I'll be looking for you.

Say yes.

BV

I let loose a few words I needed to brush off from my sorority days. This guy was unbelievable. A few weeks out from getting married, definitely "life-altering stuff," and he wanted one more quick fling before tying the knot? One more romp before saying "I do?" This guy was shameless.

I tossed my phone back into my purse and gunned it when the light turned green. Oh, I'd be there, all right. I'd be there with my phone and its camera and its voice memo recording every word under the table so that Willow would be forced into admitting I was right. She would hate it, and I hated it for her, but I would have proof. Irrefutable proof that would put this whole thing to rest and send Beau and his lies and his sketchy business ventures and his trolling for women back to where he emerged from under his rock.

I'd be there and, man, would he be sorry.

✦　✦　✦

Okay, so all the bravado I'd felt when gunning my car down Main Street had fully evaporated by the time I sat, fingering the buttons on my coat, a few blocks away from Topped Off, the coffee shop Beau had requested for our meeting place. I watched the traffic come in and out of the shop, men and women in scarves and hats that obscured their faces. I had arrived about ten minutes early, hoping to catch of glimpse of Beau as he went into the shop, but I hadn't spotted him yet. The clock on my dash said it was time. And I put my hand on the door handle, hesitating only a moment before getting out of the car and striding for the front door. I ducked into the warm room, enveloped instantly in warmth and the heady aroma of coffee. I scanned the room quickly, looking at the tables nearest me, then along the sides of an enormous coffee roaster that was slowly spinning a vat of coffee beans.

He wasn't here.

Oh, the hits just kept on coming, I fumed silently, letting my purse drop onto a chair at a table by the window. He calls an emergency meeting, talks with breathless impatience about how we needed to seize the day, and then he shows up late. I unpeeled my scarf from around my neck and sat down heavily, eyes on the door. I sat, brooding for a good five minutes and was just about to stand up, gather my things and leave, when I saw him. From my vantage point at the window, I had a long view of the street, and I could see Beau, his shoulders hunched against the cold and his nose and mouth tucked into the upturned collar of this coat. But it was unmistakably him making his way down the street from about a block away. My heart skipped a beat and I felt a new rush of anger course through my veins. I kept my eyes trained on him, shaking my head as he came closer. This man had nerves of steel, I mused as he walked with a spring in his step toward the shop. I squinted and gasped aloud when I saw he was whistling. Whistling before the kill, I supposed. Like Captain von Trapp mixed with a great white shark. I swallowed the acid creeping up my throat and got ready to let loose on the man who was conning my friend into a marriage doomed to fail.

Beau had paused on the opposite side of the street and was waiting to cross when the shape of a figure standing close to me interrupted my thoughts. I looked up to see a man standing at my table, shifting his weight from one foot to another and looking so nervous, I feared he might start to cry.

He straightened the cardigan he was wearing and cleared his throat. "Um, Liz?"

I shook my head, turning back to the window. Beau was still waiting to cross. "Sorry," I said. "You have the wrong person."

"Are you sure? Because it's okay if you're nervous. I sure am." The man's voice cracked in the last sentence.

"My name isn't—" I stopped. *Liz. Lizzie. Oh. No.* I looked up slowly and met the gaze of the man. Same brown eyes, same impish smile, and an obscene amount of hair product. "You don't look like your photo," I said weakly.

He snorted a laugh. "True enough, but you don't either. Don't worry," he said hurriedly. "I like the real version even better."

Ew. Beau had his hand on the door to the shop and he pulled hard against the breeze. When he entered, he scanned the room and settled quickly on me. I gulped. His face tensed and he waved quickly before walking up to the counter and getting in line to order.

"May I?" Cardigan Beau gestured to the empty chair but didn't wait for permission. "Gosh, my hands are shaking. This dating thing isn't for wimps." Another laugh-snort and a hopeful look to me.

"Listen, I think we have a misunderstanding," I began.

"Wait," he said. "Don't say it yet. Please. Let's just give it a chance. I know I'm not the hunk in my profile photo, but I have a lot of redeeming qualities. I know how to play guitar!" The words were rushing out of his mouth. "And I have a good job. Well, it's not really that good, it's definitely middle management, but I pay all my bills on time. And I know how to read! And I have really good table manners. All things that single women love, right?"

I glanced at the counter and saw Beau had reached the front of the line and was ordering. "Beau, listen."

He looked confused. "It's Brian."

I took a deep breath from my comfy position down in the abyss. "Right. Brian. Listen, I'm married."

"Oh." That stopped him up short. "Well," he said slowly, "that's not what I was thinking. I suppose that could be a problem."

"Yes, I'm afraid it is."

"Though," he said with a shrug, "I guess if you're okay with it, I'm okay with it. Those lines are getting pretty blurry these days."

I recoiled. "The lines are not blurry. The lines are dark. With stop signs on them. In permanent marker." All my metaphors were getting scrambled in my hurry to point to the lines.

Brian sniffed. "Don't get all preachy. You're the one who's married and trolling for a new boyfriend on a Christian dating site."

I pursed my lips and looked over to where Beau was gathering napkins and a stir straw. "I think we're done here. I'm sorry for the mix-up."

"Me too," he said, standing. His face had fallen into a frown. Reaching over to shake my hand, he said, "Nice to meet you, Liz. I hope you find what you're looking for."

I took his hand. "You, too, Brian. Good luck."

He sighed. "You were Match Number Twelve. Things aren't looking very lucky." He walked away quickly, head down, and pushed open the door to the outside. Beau was on his heels but at the last second, he turned toward me and walked to my table.

"Heidi, I know you're not my biggest fan, but will you do me a huge favor and just not mention to Willow that you saw me here?" His normally confident demeanor had been swallowed by an expression of doubt on his face. "I love her coffee, really I do, but she can't make a latte like these people. I'm sorry. I know it sounds disloyal." He shook his head, looking miserable.

I opened my mouth. Shut it.

"You know what?" he said. "Never mind. I'll tell her myself. Lying to your wife is no way to start a marriage. We'll just have to face the fact that we don't have similar tastes in coffee, even if it's painful." He laughed, his eyes lighter already. "I'm glad I ran into you. You're forcing me to face the truth." Backing toward the door he took a small sip of his drink and his eyes rolled back a bit in pleasure. "So, so good. Hey," he said, pausing, his back on the glass. "Willow said you two were meeting this morning. How'd it go?"

I stared, trying to push together all my racing thoughts into something that resembled a sentence. "This morning. Yes. We met. It was, um, interesting."

He laughed as he pushed open the door, letting in a whip of cold air. "With Willow it always is." He waved as he left and I saw the spring return to his step as he traced his path back down the block.

I watched him go until I couldn't see him anymore.

22

Our Park was as close to deserted as I'd ever seen it. I passed one solitary mom and her toddler when I crossed the playground. The mom stood with arms crossed, hat pulled down, gloved fingers gripping a coffee carafe from which puffs of steam rose. She smiled at me as I walked by, and I did my best to return the favor but was fairly certain I only made it as far as a grimace. Her son's shouts for his mom to watch him slide, watch him run, watch him spin had followed me as I walked to our bench, my shoes padding quietly over the damp earth. Green grass still stretched hopefully under a covering of leaves, but it had to know that it was doomed. The chill in the air, the dew still not burned off in the middle of the day, the tepid sunlight reaching through a thin layer of clouds: everything pointed in a straight line to eminent winter.

I lowered myself carefully onto the bench after taking a swipe at the smattering of water droplets that made perfect, tiny bubbles on the seat. The lake was glass. A perfect, upside down reflection of the shore looked up from the smooth surface, and I stared for long minutes at the play of color, light, water, and sky. The quiet was absolute. I could hear myself breathing.

My heart and stomach felt heavy within my tired frame. I tried to piece together the puzzle that had brought me to a park bench in the middle of the day, alone in every sense, feeling miserable and disoriented. I took stock of my situation and my people:

1. Annie and James—hurt and offended when I went off about the jeans. Why did I go off about the jeans? What difference did it make to me if they put their kid in jeans or a muumuu? What was *that* all about? Also, I never returned Annie's calls and barely returned her texts.

2. Willow—hurt and offended that I had undertaken an investigation on her behalf without actually mentioning it to her. Felt like I hadn't trusted her with figuring Beau out on her own. She was right. I hadn't trusted her. I gripped the cell phone within my pocket and wanted to toss it into the lake, for all the good its technology had brought me.

3. Beau—thought I despised him. Wasn't far off on the impression, but turns out, it was unmerited. Sure, he'd made a mess of his life. But at one point, I'd been all sorts of lip service about the kind of God I served and the kinds of messes He cleaned up. I swallowed hard. Beau was trying to clean up his mess and I wasn't letting him.

4. Jake. I stopped. Jake who loved me despite my vitriol and my uncertainty and my unwillingness to commit or to talk or to dive deep. My eyes stung with tears, not because of Jake's patience with me, or the kindness with which he treated me, or the way he had given me so much space and so much time and so many ups and downs with how I had approached our infertility and our desire for another baby. Those were all beautiful things, undeserved things, and I knew to be grateful for them.

But they weren't what was making my spine curl into itself, what was making me start to shake with the effort of controlling a sob. I was crying big, fat, rolling tears because all I could picture was the way he still stopped, mid sentence, and would say to me with a goofy grin, "You're so beautiful," almost always on a day when I felt distinctly unbeautiful. And because of how, when we had visited my elderly grandma that summer, Jake had sat for an entire hour after everyone else lost interest and helped Nana with the blank spaces in her crossword puzzle. And how I'd found him last week in the dim light of Nora's room, kneeling by the bed while she slept. He'd stayed there for long minutes, and I'd watched him from the doorway. When he finally stood and walked quietly out of the room, he'd been startled to see me there. He'd brushed tears from his cheeks and said gruffly that'd he'd been praying for his little girl and that sometimes it weighed heavily on him to help lead her into a tough world.

This is why I was crying. Strike that. I was blubbering. Blubbering on a park bench on a damp and frigid day and feeling like the bottom layer of sludge in the lake before me. This was no halfhearted cry session. I was fully committed: head in hands, sharp intakes of air when I got around to it, snot running into my mouth. I was a sight. No one hosted a pity party like I did that day. I was the Grand Vizier of all pity parties, which is a solitary honor to be enjoyed alone. So when I spotted a figure quickly making its way around the nearest bend in the lake path, I groaned through a sniffle. My choices were to get up and walk away, back to my car and back to my real life, which sounded distinctly horrible, or I could wait it out, bury myself into my coat and pretend I was invisible. I chose the latter.

The figure was a woman, and she was very petite. Her legs, however, made up in speed what they lacked in stature. The woman was motoring toward me and had reached me within a minute. I kept my eyes, puffy though they were, fixed on the lake in front of me, tucking my chin and nose into my scarf. I needed a tissue in a bad way, but I waited until she passed before rummaging in my pockets to find one that looked mostly unused. "Mostly unused" was the best a mom could hope for in a tissue, and I found one. I raised it to my face and just about jumped out of my skin when I heard my name spoken just behind me.

"Heidi?"

I whipped around and saw the petite woman who must have circled back while I was searching for the Kleenex. It was Moira, and she was peering out from under a russet knit hat. Her brown eyes were large and concerned.

She took a step toward me. "I don't want to bother you. In fact, I tried walking by and not saying anything. But I've seen women weep a lot in my line of work and, well," she shrugged, "sometimes they want to be alone and sometimes they very much want not to be alone." She smiled sadly. "Which kind are you?"

The words were on my tongue, the ones to send her way, the ones that would deftly proclaim I was fine, just having a rough morning, that I could handle it, that there was nothing to worry about. But those words were swallowed by a fresh wave of hot tears. I saw Moira through my blurred vision and I said nothing, just moved over on the bench to make room for her.

True to her claims, this was not Moira's first rodeo. The woman knew how to let a person cry. She held my mittened hand in hers and said nothing for a long time, just waiting while I endured the latest wave. Seeing her brought up all sorts of things, but the emotion that rose like acid in my throat was grief. I was grieving. When I could finally speak, I said so.

"I thought I'd get pregnant again," I said, allowing myself to admit it for the first time out loud. "Before adopting, I mean. Before we ended up signing any papers or having a home visit or anything else that made it real."

Moira nodded. "Not unreasonable at all. It's happened many times. It could still happen."

I groaned. "Don't say that. I can't hold out any more hope just to have it crushed."

She was silent before answering. "What's wrong with hope?"

I shook my head. "It disappoints. It's fickle and untrustworthy and it hurts."

Moira nodded. "That's true. All of it. But hope also propels and inspires and builds good things from devastating things. In my experience, it's worth the risk."

"I don't want to invite her to Thanksgiving dinner," I blurted.

Moira met my gaze, confusion in her eyes. "Who?"

I swallowed. "The baby's birth mother. I can't have her over for dinner."

Moira shook her head. "You don't need to have her over for dinner. For Thanksgiving or any other time."

"I don't?" My voice sounded as tired as I felt.

"No," she said. "Your relationship with the birth mother is something on which you both agree. It's different for every family, but most birth mothers do not want to come over for dinner. They are looking for a permanent and healthy family for their child and are courageous enough to know they can't offer such a family. They instinctively understand that some distance is good for everyone."

I sat still, taking in her words, watching a red-winged blackbird land in the rushes nearby and fluff its feathers against the cold.

"Heidi, it's normal to feel scared." The kindness in Moira's voice made my heart hurt. "Feeling scared doesn't mean you aren't a good adoptive mom. You're a great mom." She smiled and beautiful, hard-won lines settled around her bright eyes. "I have a good sense about these things."

I listened to the blackbird scold us for a minute and then I took in a long, shaky breath. "Okay. Thank you."

Moira nodded and stood. "You know where to find me. Or I can always find you sitting on a bench, but maybe let me know ahead of time so I can go for my walk when you're here. It's funny," she said, adjusting her hat over her ears. "I never walk at this hour. I'm a very early morning person. But today I missed my walk and when I had a canceled appointment, I decided to venture out into the cold." She smiled. "God is so good to involve Himself in our details, isn't He?"

I nodded, watching her walk away. I felt my heart warm up and become pliable in a way that I hadn't felt in far too long, and I knew in that moment that the thaw had happened because I was finally surrendering. Surrendering to hope and to a God who could handle my doubt and my fear and even my anger that He wasn't acting according to the memos I kept sending Him. I closed my eyes, and when I sat long enough, I could feel, even through the covering of clouds and the beginning of winter's chill, the warmth of a stubborn, tenacious sun.

23

I was standing under our maple tree when the final bell rang and Nora came walking, shoulders down, out of school. She glanced up long enough to see me before returning her gaze to the ground just in front of her. Just after nearly colliding with an enormous man-child sixth grader who I swore had a peach fuzz mustache, she reached me, eyes still downcast.

I crouched down, way down, to meet her gaze. She didn't even smile when I turned my face upside down and looked ridiculous to force her to look at me.

"Did she call you?" she finally said. She let her backpack drop to the dirt.

"She did." I took both her hands in mine. "Do you want to tell me what happened?"

She shook her head before speaking in a small, tight voice. "Just tell me what Ms. Charm said."

"She said you bonked Gus Hill on the head with a clipboard. And that you had to pull a card."

Tears were falling in earnest. "I'm so sorry," she said, throwing herself into my arms. "Only really bad kids pull cards. I'm just like Gus Hill!" She was shuddering with sobs. I let her go, knowing from very recent personal experience that sometimes what a girl needed was silence and a hug.

When Nora started to do the machine-gun stutter breath, I pulled away gently and waited until she looked at me. "You, Nora Elliott, are not a bad kid. You are a great kid and you are a gift to me and your dad. Don't you ever, ever forget it."

She shook her head. "I pulled a card."

"Yep," I said. "You did. And let me tell you, if grown-ups could pull cards, I would have a whole stack of them in my purse right now."

She narrowed her eyes at me to judge the truth in my claims. "You would?"

I nodded. "I really would. I'm thinking about forty-five cards just since the first day of school."

"Wow," she said, and couldn't hide the disappointment on her face. "That's *worse* than Gus Hill."

I sighed. "It totally is. Way worse. For one thing, I was a total jerk to you this morning when we were running late. Remember that?"

Nora nodded, her chin down.

"I'm so sorry about that, Peanut. I was freaking out about things that weren't your fault but I took it out on you."

"It's all right," she said quietly, fingering the zipper on her coat.

"So there are about five cards I've pulled, just for this morning. If we'd had a principal at our house, she would have called *you* to tattle on *me*."

She smiled a small smile.

"But listen," I said as I hoisted her backpack to my shoulder. "We can't just haul around all these cards and feel terrible about them."

"Well," Nora said, drawing out the word. She fell into step

beside me. "I actually only have one card to haul around. You have forty-five."

"Good point," I said, rolling my eyes. "My point is that it doesn't do any good to just keep schlepping around our cards, feeling bad about what we've done."

"It doesn't? Because I *do* feel really bad, and I *should* feel really bad."

I saw Nora's lip start to quiver again and I spoke quickly. "Feeling bad makes us pay attention to where we've messed up. Which is a good thing. But if all we do is feel bad, nothing good comes out of it. Plus, there's Jesus."

"What does He have to do with it?" Nora said as she scurried with me across the street. Crazy carpooler in a Volkswagen nearly ran us down before we could make it to the other side.

"He has everything to do with it," I said. "We talk all the time about how God loves us, right?"

"Right." Nora sounded very sure about that one.

"Well, if that's true, than we have to act like it. Which means if we mess up and pull cards we have to remember that God still loves us. That part doesn't change. Ever."

Nora took my hand and studied the ground in front of us as we walked, but she said nothing.

"And," I continued, "since God loves us no matter what, we can do the right thing with our cards. Two things, actually. First, we ask God to forgive us for messing up big-time."

"I already did that," Nora said with a lip quiver. "He probably hated that conversation."

"No way," I said, shaking my head. "He loved it. Remember? The love part doesn't change."

We took turns jumping to the dry edges around a huge puddle on the sidewalk. Usually Nora would be squealing and giving a play-by-play of her jump but this time she moved carefully and without commentary. Discussing the propitiation of sin could do that to a girl.

"So we ask God to forgive us, which He promises always to do. And then there's Part Two."

"What's Part Two?" Nora asked, and I felt myself mirroring the dread in her voice.

"Part Two is asking forgiveness from the people we hurt."

"Noooo," Nora moaned. "That's Gus Hill for my card. And it's forty-five people for yours! We'll never finish! And I can't talk to Gus Hill!" She was stomping now, burning up the road between me and our house. "Gus Hill is annoying and mean and nasty and he hates me and he picks his boogers and he won't want to talk to me."

The asking God for forgiveness with a trembling lip was sounding like easy street compared to Part Two.

I caught up to her on the bottom step of our porch. Turning her shoulders around to face me, I said, "All of that might be true. But we still have to ask for forgiveness."

"Why?" she said, and I could see glimpses of tweendom in the look of defiance on her face.

I shrugged. "Because God told us to. And because it makes us free."

She narrowed her eyes. "We're already free. The Emancipation Proclamation. Remember?"

I honestly could not get a handle on what, exactly, was happening under the instructional wing of that woman.

"I mean heart free." Work with me, here, sis, I thought, wholly regretting my attempt at talking theology. Slippery slope. "Get rid of the cards, say we we're sorry, get our hearts free again."

I thought I'd lost her, judging by the way she ran into the kitchen and threw open the cupboard to extract a granola bar. I leaned up against the kitchen counter and chewed on my bottom lip. My forty-five cards were weighing me down, and I wanted to get rid of them. Pronto.

I opened my mouth to tell Nora my plan when she looked at me, all business. "Okay. I'm ready for Part Two. Can we do it together?"

I smiled. "I was hoping you'd say that."

✦ ✦ ✦

Our first stop was Annie and James's house. Nora and I walked up the brick pavers leading to the front door. Nora held small basket we had lined with an orange and white polka dot cloth. The polka dots hugged a half dozen chocolate peanut butter cup cookies, still a little warm from our oven.

"Wow," Nora said as her eyes swept over the lawn. "Aunt Annie doesn't have even one teeny tiny leaf on her front yard. She must rake it all the time."

"Aunt Annie likes things neat. She likes neat teeth at her work and neat grass at her house." I bit back a comment about how her neat life was about to take a nosedive into total chaos and that we should wait until next year at this time to see how her perfect lawn looked. Just bit it back, that comment. My personal growth was astonishing.

We reached the front door and I nodded when Nora looked at me, her finger paused at the doorbell.

"Part Two," I said.

She nodded and pushed the button. "You can do it," she said, eyes on the front door.

It took a minute but Annie got to the door. I waved when

she looked through the glass panes framing either side. When she opened the door, I could see the wariness on her face.

"It's the Elliott girls," she said, opening the door and motioning for us to enter. "Come in out of the cold."

Nora handed her the basket. "We made you cookies."

"Thank you," Annie said, taking the basket. She wore a fitted top and my heart leapt into my throat to see how much her belly had grown since the last time I'd really looked. Annie buried her nose in the basket and took a deep inhale. "Mmm," she said. "I smell chocolate and sugar and peanut butter. I can't think of any better things to smell."

Nora looked at me from the side hug Annie was bestowing. My daughter, never one for subtlety, cleared her throat long enough and loudly enough to fulfill the requirements for a community theater audition. "Har-harm. Har-harm!"

"Annie, I'm sorry," I said, clutching the package I held. "I haven't been a good friend to you lately and I'm very, very sorry." I could feel my shoulders inching up toward my ears, I was so tense. "I am so excited you're pregnant. Really. I'm sorry I let my hurt and anger seep into our friendship. You don't deserve it."

Annie threw her arms around me. "I should have been more sensitive," she said into my hair. "You've always despised designer denim. And I shouldn't have talked about the baby so much."

"No, that's the point," I said firmly, nudging her away so she could see my face. "You *should* talk about the baby. We are totally talking about the baby. And I am going to start talking to the baby through the nonexistent fat on your belly so your baby knows my voice before he or she even exits the womb."

Nora walked over to Annie and pressed her nose against the roundness in front. "Hello, baby. This is Nora. You will love me the most. I can braid hair." She looked up at Annie, smug. "Like that. We will brainwash your baby."

Annie laughed. "Sounds good. I approve of your brainwashing, but only because I love you so much." She leaned down to kiss Nora on the head, then over to kiss my cheek. "Thank you for coming. And thank you for the cookies. I'll be hiding them from James." Her eyes shone and I felt the lightness in my heart travel to my head. Freedom felt good.

"One more thing," I said as I stepped toward the door. I ran my fingers along the brown paper covering the object in my hands. I could feel the familiar ridges and bumps and knew this was the last time they would be mine. Offering the package to Annie, I smiled. "This is for you. I used to think it was for me, but I know better now. You can open it when I'm gone. I'll tell you the whole story another day."

She looked at the package in her hands and held it still, as if it might break.

"It's really not fragile," I said, and I followed Nora onto the front walk. "It took me awhile to figure that out, but it's true. It's not fragile at all."

Annie held the package to her chest and waved good-bye as we got into the car and pulled away from her house.

"What did you give Aunt Annie, Mom?" Nora said, her face turned toward the sun, which was starting to dip low along the tree line.

"A blanket." I turned onto the street leading back into town. "I made it a long time ago, when we were first wanting another baby after you. It's pretty and soft and perfect for a baby, but not our baby. It needs a new home. It needs a fresh start."

I got through that entire little speech without one tear. Again with the personal growth! I was crushing it!

Nora nodded, eyes still on the changing light. "Fresh starts are good. I like them."

"Speaking of, are you ready for yours?" I glanced at Nora in the rearview mirror and saw her jaw tighten.

"Not really," she said deliberately, "but we should probably take turns. You went first. So I'll go." She looked at me, eyebrows raised. "But there will be no kissing. Only Aunt Annie can kiss during her Part Two."

"Agreed," I said, pulling into the driveway of a white two story with red shutters. "In Room 12 we keep our kisses to ourselves," I said in my best kindergarten singsong.

Nora shot a disapproving glance at me as she reached across the back seat to grab another basket of cookies. "Mom, that's disgusting. We do not talk about kissing at school. Or guns."

I followed her lead as she got out of the car. Her pace walking up to the front door was just under that of a geriatric sloth. "Um, Norie?" I said when she stopped to inspect an ant crawling into a crack on the sidewalk. "We're going to miss Christmas if you walk any more slowly."

She sighed and stood to her full height. "Are you sure this is Gus Hill's house?"

"Yep," I said. "Got the address right out of our brand new student directory. Gus Hill lives here with his mom, his dad, his two older brothers, and his pet goldfish, Snuggles."

Her eyes widened. "He has a goldfish?"

"Not sure about that part," I said, prodding her gently along with a hand on her tiny shoulder blades. "But you can ask him about Snuggles after you give him the cookies."

In due time, and by that I mean just before I lost my mind, we reached the front door, and I rang the doorbell before Nora could turn tail and run. A harried-looking woman answered the door. Her blonde needed retouching and was in no way obeying the confines of the ponytail into which it was gathered.

"Yes?" she said through the screen door.

"Hi," I said. "I'm Heidi Elliott and this is my daughter, Nora." I waited for Nora to speak but she seemed to have entered some sort of catatonic shock and was staring, motionless, at the woman's right elbow.

I cleared my throat. "Nora and Gus are in the same class at school."

Hardness flickered in the woman's eyes. "What did he do?"

"Oh," I said hurriedly. "Nothing. I mean, not that I know of anyway." Except for blazing the first steps on a path directly leading straight to juvey, I thought but wisely omitted from the conversation. "Nora would like to talk to Gus. Is he home?"

"Gus!" the woman called in a voice so shrill and practiced, it made the hair on my arms stand up. "Front door!"

In a moment, Gus came sliding down the cluttered hallway in his socks. When he saw Nora, he stopped. "What's she doing here?"

Oh, Gus, I thought. Never greet a pretty girl with a snarl. I could pretty much guarantee that once he hit high school and figured out he needed a date to homecoming, he would regret that pattern.

"Gus," Nora said, her voice suddenly strong. Something about seeing that boy riled her up. "I made you cookies. And I want to say I'm sorry for bonking you on the head during school today. You made me supermad, but I still shouldn't have bonked you. Violence is never the answer."

Gus stared at my daughter blankly. I glanced at his mom and saw her frowning in a way that made me think this kind of thing was new for her.

"What kind of cookies are they?" Gus finally asked.

"Chocolate peanut butter cup," Nora said, her shoulders relaxing. "Here." She held out the basket and Gus opened the door.

"Thanks," he said, looking suddenly unsure of himself. "I usually hate peanut butter stuff but these smell good."

Nora grinned. "My mom and I made them. Don't forget to wash your hands before you eat."

I winced, knowing well the trials and travails of being a bossy firstborn girl. Hand-washing instructions were part of our DNA.

"Thank you." Gus's mom was looking at Nora. "It was very grown-up of you to bake treats for Gus and even more grown-up to apologize. I didn't even know you'd had a problem at school."

Nora shrugged one shoulder. "That's Okay. My mom has lots of people to apologize to. Gus is my only one, so it wasn't any trouble."

Gus's mom pressed her lips together but not before I saw her smile. "I see. Well, it's good to admit when you've screwed up. I wish more people would do it."

We said our good-byes but not until Nora had reminded Gus to bring a leaf or acorn in for science the next day. "And don't bring a brown leaf," she called from our car. "We'll have too many of those already."

By the look on Gus's face, I could see he had fully acquired the gift of tuning out a female voice.

"Good job, kid," I said as I turned the key in the ignition. "How do you feel?"

"Way better," Nora said. She let her head fall back on the car seat. "I still don't want to watch him eat his boogers, but my heart feels better." She sighed. "Phew. I'm hungry. What's for dinner?"

I rolled my eyes. "Haven't made it. I've been too busy saying sorry to everyone. Let's go pick up some tacos to take home to Dad."

Nora cheered and did some sort of neck dance.

"I just have one more stop." I passed the elementary school and drove a well-worn route to Willow's house. "It won't take long."

"That only makes two cards," Nora said from the back seat. "Your math is bad, Mom."

"I figure about ten to Annie and ten to Willow," I reasoned aloud. "And the last twenty-five are for Dad."

Nora was humming, the new lightness in her chest much more interesting than her mother's addition problem. As promised, the stop at Willow's was brief. I left the basket of cookies and a sealed letter on one of the rocking chairs on her front porch. I didn't ring the doorbell but I did text her when we got to the Taco House.

"Special delivery," I typed. "Check your porch."

I pushed to send and tucked my phone in my pocket. Two down, one to go, I thought as we waited in line to order. Part Two wasn't complete, but for the first time in days, I thought I'd be able to eat a meal and begin to fill the gnawing feeling in my stomach. Freedom tasted good.

24

The season's first snow began in earnest just after dinner. We were doing the few dishes we'd dirtied with a meal of takeout burritos when Nora exclaimed, "It's snowing!" She dumped the plate she was carrying into the sink, sending up a splash of water and soap bubbles. "Sorry!" she said, making absolutely no indication she felt one bit apologetic, and she rushed to the front door, heaved it open and ran out onto the porch.

"Come look! Mom! Dad! You're going to miss it!"

Jake sniffed the sniff of the cynical. "Not likely," he muttered. "Unless I fall asleep until the end of April."

"Now, now," I said, linking my arm in his. "We can't be old and crusty Midwesterners yet. We're still in our thirties."

He held the front door for me, and I noticed his polite courtesy was still in fine form. Avoiding my gaze, he said, "Thirty is the new eighty, haven't you heard?" He smiled at Nora, who was running out from under the porch awning and squealing as the snow covered her hair and shoulders.

"We should make her put on shoes. And a coat," I said, watching her.

"Nah," Jake said. "Those are for sissies. Not for hardened Midwesterners."

We stood shoulder to shoulder, watching our daughter and the snow as it picked up streetlight and sparkled coming down. At this rate, our town would be enveloped in white by morning. I reached over, eyes still on Nora, and took Jake's hand. He didn't pull away, but it was a noncommittal hand-holding. He held on but barely and then abruptly pulled away and clapped his hands once.

"It's getting chilly standing here. I'm going to put down some salt, make a first pass with the shovel. You good with doing bedtime?" He was already back in the house and calling from the entryway.

"Sure," I said, nodding, a plan forming and making my heart skip. "Norie," I said. She looked up from the miniscule snowball she was attempting to form with her fingers. "Two more minutes, sister. It's time for bed." I shook my head as she began to protest. "Nope. Tomorrow will be more fun anyway with more snow. And a coat. And snowpants."

I walked to the bathroom, started Nora's bath, and strode to her room to draw the shades and extract clean pj's from the jumbled pile of clothes in her drawers. I did everything I could to speed up the process, even squeezing toothpaste onto her toothbrush and placing it carefully on the side of the sink. I walked to the front of the house and knocked on the living room window, motioning for Nora to come in. Hurry, I thought, watching her meander slowly up to the front door and shake the snow out of her hair. The clock is ticking, I thought, and I've waited long enough.

✦ ✦ ✦

I heard the garage door close, and then Jake banging around, hanging the shovel on its hook, stomping out his boots on the rug. I grabbed the plate and rushed to the living room, making sure again that the shades were drawn. The last thing I needed was the Havershams dropping by for a surprise visit and helpful advice on technique.

I laid the plate carefully on the coffee table and then sat on the couch. Then stood. Then sat. Good grief, was I bad at this kind of thing. I was in mid stand when Jake came around the corner, his hair tousled and cheeks and nose pink from the cold. He stopped, his stocking feet paused in the middle of a stride. He took a long, leisurely glance up, then down, then up again, and a slow smile started to one side of his mouth.

"You're wearing my favorite outfit," he said, a spark in his eye.

"I am," I said softly, suddenly nervous.

"And it smells really good in here."

I pointed to the plate. "I made dessert. Actually, the Johanssens made dessert at their bakery this morning and then I took them home and baked them, but." I stopped, winded with all my ridiculous words. "Yes. Butter and sugar and almond paste do smell really good together."

Jake peeled off his coat and draped it slowly across a chair, taking care to watch me as he did.

I smiled. "I'm not going to run away. You don't have to keep an eye on me."

He crossed the room and pulled me close. I shivered at the cold still on his clothes. "I like keeping an eye on you. And plus, you haven't exactly been the picture of consistent messages lately." He leaned down to kiss me on the tender spot under my earlobe. "I'm worried you'll suddenly think better of this and run to the bedroom to find your Springdale High Debate Team sweatshirt and flannel pants. That," he said quietly into my ear, "would be a tragedy."

"I was really good at debate," I said, hearing the blood start to rush in my ears. "District champs three years in a row."

"Would have been all four years if you'd worn this getup," Jake said. I could hear the smile in his voice.

"Gross," I said, but without conviction. I was feeling anything but gross.

Jake kissed my neck and began unbuttoning his shirt. I pushed him gently away and forced him to make contact with my eyes, which took awhile since he was more interested in a southern view.

"Wait," I said.

Jake moaned. "Oh, my gosh. It's like dating all over again."

I laughed. "Not exactly. This time I'm a sure thing."

"Good," he said, and I heard the growl in his voice.

"Listen," I said.

"Nah," he said. "We can do that part later." He leaned toward me and I moved back a step, laughing.

"I need to say something," I insisted. "Should I put on a robe?"

"No," he said with a sullen expression. "A robe is worse than flannel pants."

I took his hands. "I'm so sorry, Jake."

He watched my face as the words tumbled out.

"I'm sorry for my mixed messages. I'm sorry I wasn't totally honest with you about my misgivings and insecurities and worries. I felt like I'd already disappointed you so much with my inability to carry a baby—"

"Heidi," he warned.

I put up a hand. "I know you didn't feel like that, but I was very busy listening to lies that were not true about myself. I couldn't even hear what you were saying." I took a deep breath. "I love you so much, it hurts. I love that you are fully committed to me, and not just when I'm wearing this hooker outfit."

"Hey," he said with a frown, "don't disrespect the outfit. Or hookers."

"And I love it that you make me laugh and hold the door for me and bring me flowers and ask me about my day and assume I can do anything, even adopt a baby and be a good mom to that baby."

My voice caught but I pressed on. "I really don't know what I'm doing and I'm still scared. But I know now that being scared is normal. In fact, maybe a little healthy fear is the best way to remember I'm not in control of the universe. And that the God who loves me with a ferocious love won't let me go, even when I'm about to wet my pants."

"But not in this outfit, right? Because that would be a shame." Jake looked very serious but I saw the mischief in his eyes.

I put my arms around his neck and kissed him like I meant it. I *did* mean it, so there was no struggle there. "Do you forgive me?" I said when we came up for air.

"Forgive. Yes." Jake kissed the indentation of my collarbone.

"Will you still adopt a baby with me? Even though I was fickle and irritating and unsure?"

"Baby. Lots of babies." Jake lifted me off my feet and carried me to the bedroom, never pausing in his pursuit of my shoulders, my lips, my neck.

"Can I have a new Mercedes-Benz?" I said.

"Yes."

"And a trip to the Caribbean?"

"Book it tomorrow."

"And a kitchen remodel?"

"Appliances too."

I laughed as he laid me on the bed and joined me there, the look on his face and the urgency of his touch assuring me that all was forgiven, we were fully ourselves again, and that dessert was definitely going to have to wait.

25

It was Saturday, four weeks later, and I was washing the breakfast dishes with a care they did not merit. Jake came up behind me at the sink and wrapped his arms around me to still my hands from their repetitive scrubbing.

"You've been at that dish for four minutes. I timed you."

I frowned. "Timing me is weird."

"Not as weird as four full minutes on a clean plate."

Nora rounded the corner and scowled. "Stop kissing and hugging. We have an emergency."

She stomped away and I turned a half circle toward Jake, who kept his arms firmly encircling my waist. "You smell good," I said into his neck, kissing it for good measure. "I think our daughter is sick of the way we're always pawing at each other lately. We should go back to angry and repressed. I think she preferred that."

He kissed me long and slow. "Are you sure?" he asked and I promise I would have forgotten all of my dignity right then and there if Nora hadn't called from her room.

"Mom! I need you. Right. Now. I'm freaking out!"

Jake made a face. "She's too young to use the word 'freaking.'"

I laughed. "She comes by freaking naturally. Have you met her mother?"

I could feel Jake watching me as I walked away and I shook my head at how ridiculous we were being, acting like high school sweethearts who couldn't get enough of each other. Marriage, it turned out, had all sorts of ups and downs. The ups were particularly delicious.

"Okay," I said, hands on hips. "Show me the tragedy."

"Today is Willow's wedding. Right?"

"Right," I said, my thoughts returning to where they'd been when I'd spent four minutes on that breakfast plate. It had been over a month since Nora and I left the cookies and my apology letter on Willow's front step. She had sent a gracious text thanking us for the effort, and she'd said she would call when she was ready to talk. After a few days, I'd stopped checking my phone compulsively. But the strain on our friendship was never far from my thoughts. Not when I opened the heavy envelope with a pretty and simple wedding invitation tucked inside; not when I drove by Willow's café and smiled to see the new potted topiaries lit up outside the door; and not when I woke that morning and felt a bone-deep sadness that Willow was getting married and I'd missed the entire, breathless engagement because I was so busy trying to control the outcome.

"Willow is getting married, which means I have to look beautiful." Nora glowered at her closet.

"No problem," I said. "You could wear a pillow case and you'd still look beautiful."

Nora rolled her eyes.

At her mother.

Nora was in kindergarten.

I was doomed.

Forty-five minutes later, I was still in Nora's bedroom, slouched against the wall and trying for the fifth time to explain why a feather boa was not a great choice for wedding attire and that it would detract from the beauty of the bride, which was our primary visual focus at such an event. Nora had flopped down on her bed, entangled with a pink boa that had lost half its feathers in an unfortunate vacuuming incident. I let my head drop into my hands and was trying to come up with a plan that would allow me to go to my own closet and plot what I was going to wear, when I heard the doorbell ring. I assumed it was the mailman dropping off the Saturday delivery, but Jake's voice was too warm and familiar to be greeting our mailman, an irritable gentleman named Marlon who hated dogs, children, and weather.

I pulled myself to my feet and was met by Jake in the doorway. His eyes were buggy. "It's Willow," he said in an excited whisper. He glanced at Nora and seeing her fist pump and scramble to her feet, he said, "Kiddo, you're in here with me. Mommy and Willow have to talk privately."

"What?" Disbelief registered dropped Nora's mouth into an open O. "I can't see the bride? On her wedding day? This place is just like jail!"

Jake moved aside to let me pass through the doorway and I closed the door and Nora's wailing behind me. Willow was waiting for me on the couch. Her wild curls had been tamed and pinned in a loose, pretty bun at the nape of her neck. She looked up at me, eyes shining.

"You look stunning," I said. "Every bit the beautiful, blushing bride."

She smiled but it looked like her heart wasn't in it. "The hair and makeup look good but my heart is hammering in my chest like some wacked-out percussion ensemble." She smoothed her coat with her hands. Bell-bottom jeans and bright red clogs stood out against her tailored cream wool coat. You could put the hippie in winter white bridal mode but the hippie would remain.

Willow cleared her throat and looked me full in the face. "Heidi, I need your help. And I need to say I'm sorry. Which should I do first?"

I bit back a smile, unaccustomed to seeing Willow at a loss for words. "Check off the apology because I'm the one who owes you, not the other way around."

She shook her head so hard I was concerned her updo would suffer. "No. That's wrong. I've been telling myself that for a month and I woke up this morning knowing that was a pile of crap. Oops." She put a gloved hand over her mouth. "Sorry. I shouldn't say that word with Nora here."

I laughed, already feeling the weight in my heart begin to lift. "She's heard a tidge worse, I assure you."

"Well, then, it was crap. I've been walking with Jesus for a very long time, and I don't know what got into me that I thought I was excused from ready forgiveness. He surely has never been stingy with me in that regard." Her eyes shone as she crossed the room to hug me. "Please forgive me for taking so long to say I forgive you. I was pouting. Even old women can pout."

I held onto her, being careful not to muss her curls. "Absolutely, one hundred percent forgiven. We shall never speak of it again."

She bit her cheek and then said, "Can't I call you Nancy Drew? Just every now and then."

"No, thanks."

"How about Da Vinci Code?"

"Never."

"Jason Bourne?"

I frowned. "There is no way you've seen Jason Bourne movies."

She straightened her spine, trying to look indignant. "I read the books. And I *might* see them, now that Beau is bringing Netflix to the marriage." She stopped, eyes big. "Beau! That reminds me. I need your help with Beau."

I shook my head. "I don't think so. I think I've done quite enough, thanks. My help with Beau hasn't been very helpful."

Willow retrieved a crumpled piece of paper from her coat pocket. "No, I mean it. These are my vows." She opened the paper and I glimpsed her elongated, angular script. "And I want to put one part in Spanish. But, um, I don't speak Spanish." She sighed. "Maybe that's dumb. I've waited so long. It's too late, right? To learn how to say it well enough so that he'll understand I'm speaking Spanish and not pig latin?"

"Not at all," I said, walking her to our kitchen table. "We'll keep it simple. And we'll practice it enough so you feel comfortable." I grinned. "He's going to love it."

She smiled, her face light and young. "He will. Even if I butcher it. Maybe especially if I butcher it. He's just that kind of guy."

We sat down and got to work writing words of love and promise and joy to a man who I knew now, without a doubt, was a man who deserved such things.

✦ ✦ ✦

Willow was trilling her r's on the way out our front door when she stopped and let out a little cry. "I almost forgot!" She rushed out to her car and came back moments later carrying a poofy white bag by the hanger. "Nora!" she called.

Nora, who had likely been listening by her door, was in the entryway before her name had stopped echoing off the walls. She buried her face in Willow's legs and said, "You're getting married. You're a *bride*."

"That I am," Willow said. "And do you know what? I am in desperate need of a flower girl. I don't suppose you're free this afternoon?"

Nora squealed and continued squealing as Willow peeled back the garment bag to reveal a frothy, girly, twirly, cream-colored flower-girl dress. With a matching boa.

I laughed and Jake looked nervous at the ease with which Nora stripped down to her days of the week underpants right there in the family room. The dress fit, the boa worked, and the two most beautiful members of the bridal party waved each other off as Jake and I stood in the doorway, feeling the cold rush into the house but not even noticing the chill.

26

St. Peter's had never looked better. The remnants of a winter afternoon sunset spilled down from the tall windows, suffusing the room with a soft glow that entered a kind of dance with the hundreds of candles that lined the window ledges, the altar, the weathered stone stairs leading to the lectern. A cellist sat to one side of the stairs, playing unaccompanied Bach, the notes warming and filling the room, rising to the vaulted white ceiling, echoing off the rustic wooden pews that had been placed in rows in the sanctuary. The crisp aroma of newly cut evergreen branches and winter berries was the perfect counterpoint to the white roses, tulips, and peonies that gathered at the ends of rows and in simple, stunning bouquets on the altar.

I turned in my seat and looked back at the heavy wooden doors that the ushers were allowing to close. It was time.

"Are you sure I shouldn't be back there with Nora?" I whispered for the sixteenth time to Jake.

He slipped his warm hand into mine. "Willow said to sit. She's the bride and the boss. So we sit. Besides," he said quietly, his eyes twinkling, "do you really think Nora wants you around? No offense, but this morning I believe she compared us to her two jailers."

I sighed. "We are never going to make it to eighteen."

Jake squeezed my hand as the cellist let a final note of Bach ring into the empty space. "Time for the boa."

A mandolin player joined the cellist and they started in a heart-stoppingly beautiful rendition of "Be Thou My Vision." I watched my little girl walk slowly down the aisle, the boa trailing behind her. Her smiled widened when she saw me and Jake, and I waved discreetly. Jake gave her a "rock on" signal with his hand and I could see Nora stifle the urge to return the gesture. I leaned into my husband as we watched her walk to the end of the aisle and then shake Beau's hand solemnly. Even from our spots halfway back, I could see the twinkle in Beau's eye. His formal posture and slight bow was exactly what Boa Girl was seeking. She turned, beaming, and watched the back of the room.

A muted rustle spread through the pews, and we stood to greet the bride. Willow's eyes were bright and large and beautiful. Her dress was breathtaking. The bodice was beaded in a cream fabric that picked up the candlelight as she moved. The skirt began in an empire waist and fell in pretty folds down to the floor. When she turned to smile at Blue and Stream as they led her down the aisle, I could see she wore a tiny spray of baby roses in her hair. I stood on my tiptoes to see Beau's face. He stood with tears rolling slowly down his cheeks. I was certain he'd forgotten we were all there to give witness to these moments. He saw Willow and Willow alone. Willow reached the end of the aisle and stood with all three of her boys as they kissed her in turn. She smiled, laughed a little at something Hike said, and then she fixed her eyes on Beau.

"They're good together," Jake said as I watched the sons turning to shake hands with Beau.

I nodded, blinking furiously. I had a long way to go during that service, and if I launched into the snort-cry right away, I would end up needing a hot toddy and a nap by the time we made it to the reception.

Pastor Smits greeted us, his hands outstretched under his clerical robe. "Willow and Beau have asked that we remember this is holy and joyful celebration, and that each of us is an integral part of these moments. You are here because you are deeply loved by these two people. You are here because Willow and Beau want you to mark this moment with them. They are starting something new and sacred and God-honoring, and they know we're all better together."

I closed my eyes, letting those words wash over me. Tears fell without pause down my face, and I felt Jake pull me close to him. Better with Jake, the man who loved me with all of himself. Better with Willow and Annie, friends who were ready to dig into hard things and wait for me when it was too difficult to move out of the spot that had me stuck. Better with Nora and the baby I wanted so desperately. We weren't done with that part of the story, I knew. It was going to look different than I'd planned, but I was getting the hint that Plan B was every bit as sweet and sure and good. And better with Jesus, the author and finisher of all good things, hard things, to be sure, but good nonetheless. I opened my eyes, ready to see clearly again, and breathed a prayer, reaching for Him, knowing He was not far off.

EPILOGUE

"It's here!" Nora came careening across the wood floors in her stocking feet. I winced, sure she would clip the edge of the coffee table and face-plant into the wall. She came close but pulled up at the last second. Her face was triumphant.

"See," she said in her best instructive tone. "It's perfectly safe to run in the house in my socks. Plus, it makes the dust go away." She lifted up her foot to show me a layer of gray that had settled there.

In one fell swoop I could feel relief for the preservation of my daughter's life and limbs and a deep regret that she was fit enough to insult me. I snatched the postcard from her hand.

"What does it say?" Nora asked, jumping from one foot to another. "Man, I wish I could read cursive."

"Ah, but then you would have no need of your mother," I said, pulling her onto the couch and tickling under her armpits.

She squealed. "I would too!" she said. "I'd need you to cook my dinner!"

"What else?"

"Wash my clothes!"

"What else?"

"Do all my chores!"

The tickling intensified.

"Okay, okay," she said, surrendering. "I'd need you to kiss me and hug me and get Band-Aids when I wipe out and tuck me in and say you love me."

"Exactly," I said, letting her wiggle free. "And don't you forget it."

"What's going on in here?" Jake asked. His hair was dusted with a layer of white ceiling paint after a morning of working in the spare bedroom. We'd received our first request from a birth mom to meet with us during the upcoming week. I was surprised to feel absolute calm about the idea, but Jake had roared into a frenetic home improvement mode. We were meeting the birth mom, per her request, at the Caribou Coffee on Highway 5, but somehow Jake was connecting this very preliminary conversation with the need to repaint the white ceiling . . . white.

He looked at us with mock disapproval. "I could hear you wild women through my ear buds. Vanilla Ice couldn't even compete."

I stared. "You do know his real name is Rob Van Winkle. Which sounds a little like he should be wearing a kerchief and a flannel night shirt."

Jake frowned. "I believe you're confusing him with Wee Willie Winkie. Vanilla Ice revolutionized pop music. He was a pioneer. A renegade. Very edgy. Just like me." At this point, Jake spun around in a labored, white-man dance move, ending with something that was supposed to look tough but actually looked like jazz hands.

"You certainly are edgy, in a Karen Carpenter kind of way," I said, turning to the crumpled postcard that had wedged between the couch cushions. "Nora got today's Costa Rica postcard from Willow and Beau."

"Read it! Read it!" My daughter was regressing to toddlerhood even as I watched.

I raised an eyebrow.

"Please," she said. I could see the effort on her face to slow down the train. "Please read it, I mean."

I cleared my throat and read aloud.

"*Querida* Nora,

Today we hit the open market in the small beach town near where we are staying. We had so much fun being food nerds and buying blackberries, pineapple, mango, *plátano*s, papaya, and *guanábana*. I'm trying not to eat it all at once but so far I'm not very good with self-control.

Yesterday we woke up to a terrifying sound. I thought we were either being invaded by aliens or that a wild boar had snuck into our room during the night and was hiding under the bed. I cowered like a ninny under the covers and made Beau, my fearless prince, go check the outside of our little *casita*. He walked over to the door in his underwear and—"

"Wait, wait, wait," Nora said, hand in the air. "Beau was in his underwear?"

"Apparently," I said. I could see Jake in the doorway, biting his cheek.

"And Willow saw him in his underwear?" Nora said, nose already wrinkling.

"She definitely did. And he probably saw Willow in her underwear. They're married, kiddo. Underwear is part of the deal."

Nora shuddered. "I'm never getting married. Or if I do, I will not be showing my underwear to my husband." She switched to her best Calyspo Charm voice. "Private parts are private, not for seeing or touching."

Jake laughed a lecherous laugh and I rushed to continue reading.

"Do you know what was on the doorstep?"

Nora shook her head and I read on.

"Nothing. No alien, and no boar."

Nora giggled and then said, "Oh, good. No one else saw Beau in his underwear."

I kept reading.

"However, a very loud, very snarky, very small HOWLER MONKEY was far, far up in the palm tree next to our *casita* and Beau swears he was laughing at the silly gringo who looked so nervous."

Nora looked worried. "Beau shouldn't swear, Mom. Gus Hill swore this week and he didn't even get the chance to pull a card. He had to go straight to the principal's office. No recess."

"In this case," I said, "Beau wasn't saying a naughty word."

"Though I sure might if a monkey was screaming at me," Jake muttered.

"He didn't swear," I said to Nora, one eyebrow up at my husband. "Willow means that Beau promised. No bad words."

"Phew," Nora said. "I would hate to have to tell Willow that she married a boy who makes bad choices."

"Tell me about it," I said under my breath and finished reading the postcard.

"I hope all is well in Springdale and that you miss me horribly. We will be back in two weeks, which means lots and lots of postcards for you, my dear. Thanks for being our flower girl. You looked goooorgeous, dahling. XOXO, Willow."

"Okay, now Beau's part." Nora was ready, definitely over the produce selection at the market and even the howling primate. Beau's part was her favorite.

I read Beau's scrawl at the bottom of the card, saying the words slowly so she could digest their meaning.

"What's the difference between boogers and broccoli?"

Nora scrunched up her forehead, deep in thought. "This one is tough."

I rolled my eyes. It was the fourth booger joke in four days. Beau had found his way to my daughter's heart and it was straight through her nose.

Nora shook her head. "I don't know. What's the difference?"

I made a face. "'Kids don't eat broccoli.'"

"Ewwwww!" Nora giggled. "That's so disgusting. But I like it. May be my favorite so far."

Jake scooped up Nora and dangled her by her ankles. "No way," he said. "My favorite was 'What did the booger in love say to his girlfriend?'"

"'I'm stuck on you,'" Nora shouted, barely able to say the words in between fits of giggles.

"All dignity has officially left the building," I said, frowning from my perch on the couch.

"Dignity is dumb," Jake said as he plopped Nora onto my lap. She curled into me, giggling like a fiend. "I'll show you dignity."

He ripped the earbuds out of his phone and "Ice, Ice, Baby" thumped out of the speaker. The sound was tinny, the song ridiculous, but Nora and I gave in, soon doubled over in laughter as Jake moonwalked, shimmied, and did the Worm all over the family room, the white flecks in his hair flying out on all sides as he spun and whirled.

Nora draped her arms and legs over me as we laughed. I watched my husband make a total fool of himself in order to bring his girls joy, and I knew again, to the very core of me, that this place, this life, the one we were building together, even with all its cracks and bumps and imperfections, this life was the one I needed, the one I wanted, and that best of all, it was home.

Bonus content includes:

Acknowledgments

About the Author

Sneak Peek: Sample chapters from *Stretch Marks*, a novel by Kimberly Stuart

ACKNOWLEDGEMENTS

Thank you to . . .

. . . Leah Garland for her open heart and willingness to share with me the inner workings and breathtaking beauty involved in the adoption process. Your work is a gift to so many women and babies, and to the families that form under your care.

. . . Betsy and Ryan Beach, for living a stunning story of faith, hope, and ferocious love, and to Jonah and Olivia, for going on the adventure with them and being brave all along the way. I love you four so much, it's almost ridiculous.

. . . Jenny B. Jones, for being an author who tells beautiful, funny, charming stories, and for being a friend who *lives* beautiful, funny, charming stories, and then lets me in on them. Thank you for not rolling your eyes when I ask questions like, "What's this newfangled electronic book I hear so much about?" You're my favorite guru.

. . . Jamie Chavez, my very favorite bibliophile, for making me sound far more eloquent than I am. The word *amazing* doesn't even come close.

. . . The indomitable Anna Dorfman, who can design covers that make me want to read my own darn books. You are a force, Anna, and I am grateful.

. . . Makila and Sarah, who still root for Heidi Elliott (and for the crazy woman who made her up) after all these years. Thanks for telling me to just do it. I did!

. . . My extended family for reminding me of who I am by

who we are together. I love you!

... Mom and Dad, the best of the very best. God is so good to me, even though I'm a total pain in His divine neck. He gave me you, you love me still, and you remind me every day of how to live a life worthy of the calling we have received. Nobody does life, generosity, hope, and good, worthy work like you two. I am so grateful you are mine.

... Ryan, Jen, Linds, and Jimmy, for cheering with wild abandon. Sorry about all the times I bossed you around. I was probably right, but let's not dwell on that now. Love you.

... Ana, Mitchell, and Thea for making my days full and rich and good-to-the-core. I am so, so much better because we are together.

... Marc, the reason I love to write romance. Thank you for still making my knees go wobbly, two decades into loving you. The truth of how we live—with all the bumps and bruises, all the joys and triumphs, all the rough and all the smooth—that truth is so much sweeter than fiction. I love real life with you.

ABOUT THE AUTHOR

KIMBERLY STUART lives with her husband and three children in Iowa, where she writes faithfully before laundry and during nap time. She is the author of *Balancing Act, Bottom Line, Stretch Marks, Act Two, Operation Bonnet,* and forthcoming *Sugar.* To purchase another Kimberly Stuart book or to receive a free (free!) excerpt, please visit kimberlystuart.com/books.

Sneak Peek

Sample chapters from *Stretch Marks*
a novel by Kimberly Stuart

1

UNDER THE WEATHER

Mia's nose was stuck in her own armpit. Not a lot of glamour there, but she was working toward a higher purpose.

"Think of how your organs are thanking you for acknowledging *them*, for being considerate enough to stretch *them*." Delia's voice floated from the front of the room where, Mia knew without looking, she joined the class in a binding pose that could make most grown men cry like little girls.

Mia breathed an audible breath, collecting a healthy whiff of deodorant-laced sweat. In the nose, out the nose, throat relaxed. She closed her eyes, feeling the ends of her fingers beginning to slip out of the bind. *Liver, pancreas, you're welcome,* she thought and felt her stomach make an uncharacteristic lurch. The radiator kicked in beside where she stood, infusing heat and a bass hum to the room. Mia focused on an unmoving spot on the floor and not on the spandexed and heaving tush of the woman on the mat in front of her.

"And now using the muscles in your core, slooowly release and come back to mountain pose." Delia manipulated her voice and cadence to stretch like honey. On any other day, her instructor's voice sounded like a lullaby to Mia, a quiet but persistent reminder to breathe deeply and recycle paper and plastic. Today, though, Mia felt an urge to ask Delia to speak up. She wanted concrete sounds, solid sounds; the feathery intonations landing lightly around the room made her insides itch. She pulled out of the bind and stood at the top of her mat, feet planted, palms turned outward.

"Feel better yet?" Frankie whispered to Mia from the mat next to her.

Mia sighed. "Not yet."

"Let's move into our warrior sequence." Delia modeled the correct form on her lime-green mat and the class obediently followed suit.

Four poses later Mia hadn't shaken the bug she'd hoped was just an out-of-sorts feeling to be shed with a good workout. She felt elderly, cranky. Not even downward-facing dog had brought any relief. She lay on her back during the last minutes of class, trying to melt into the floor, *be* the floor. The spandexed woman was snoring. This final pose, savasana, was intended to provide participants final moments to recover, to be still and let their minds quiet before reentering the chaos of the outside world. Most yoga aficionados soaked up the pose. In Mia's class she'd spotted a plump, permed woman wearing a sweatshirt that declared in stark black print *I'm just here for the savasana.*

Today, though, Mia couldn't keep her eyes shut. She curled and flexed her toes, wishing Delia would crank up some Stones or Black Crowes instead of the Tibetan chimes lilting out of the stereo. Her impatience with a woman who freely quoted Mr. Rogers was beginning to worry her. Even in the hush of the room, her thoughts continued in an unruly spin, and when Delia brought everyone back to lotus, Mia glimpsed a scowl on her reflection in the mirror.

"Let's just enjoy the long, strong feeling of our bodies," Delia said. Her eggplant yoga gear revealed taut muscles. "Our organs are thanking us for a good massage."

Right. Organs. Mission accomplished, Mia thought, trying to concentrate on the gratitude her body owed her. But her mind crowded with images of bloody, squishy masses, pulsating or writhing in the way organs must do, and she found herself springing from her mat and bolting to the back of the studio. She threw open the door to the ladies' room and gripped the toilet bowl in a new pose, aptly christened Riotous Retching.

✦ ✦ ✦

"Mia?" Frankie's voice was subdued, even though a post-class din was making its way through the restroom door.

Mia emerged from the stall. "I guess sun salutations weren't such a good idea." She washed her face and hands at the sink, trying not to inhale too deeply the scent of eucalyptus rising from the soap. She watched her face in the mirror, noting the pale purple circles under her eyes that persisted even with the extra sleep she'd indulged in that week. Mia smoothed her eyebrows with clammy fingers, taking care not to tug the small silver piercing, and glimpsed Frankie's concerned expression in the mirror. "Don't worry," Mia said. "I feel much better now. Must just be a virus."

Frankie handed over Mia's coat and a hemp bag proclaiming *Save the Seals.* "I'll walk you home. Let's stop at Gerry's store for soup and crackers."

Mia made a face. "Crackers, yes. Soup, definitely not."

Outside the studio, weak February sunshine played hide-and-seek with wispy cloud cover. Frankie looped her arm around Mia's waist.

Mia glanced at her friend. "I like the blue."

Frankie turned her head to showcase the full effect. "Do you? I meant for it to be more baby blue, less sapphire, but I got distracted with this crazy woman on the Home Shopping Network and left the dye on too long."

In the two years Mia had known her, Frankie had demonstrated a keen affection for adventurous hair coloring. Magenta (advent of spring), emerald green (popular in March), black and white stripes (reflecting doldrums after a breakup), now blue. The rainbow tendency endeared Frankie to Mia, who'd braved an extended though unsuccessful flirtation with dreadlocks during college, but otherwise had settled for a comparatively conformist 'do of patchouli-scented chestnut curls.

"How did this change go over with Frau Leiderhosen?"

Frankie whistled. "She *loved* it. In fact she wondered if we could have a girls' night out this weekend and take turns trading beauty secrets."

Mia snorted, which was an unfortunate and unavoidable by-product of her laughter. The snorts only encouraged Frankie.

"'But, *meine frau*,' I said, 'I can't possibly instruct the master! A mere mortal such as I? It'd be like a Chihuahua taking over the dressing room of J-Lo! Or Sophia Loren! Or Gisele Bündchen, a woman who shares with you, dear boss, an impressive German name and an uncanny sense of style!'"

"Stop it." Mia clutched her stomach and groaned. "Yoga and laughter are off limits until further notification from my digestive tract."

Frankie sighed. "I do feel sorry for her. I never should have shown up with a mousy blonde bob cut for the initial interview. I was *so* average librarian." She shook her head as they slowed near Gerry's Grocery. "Only to turn on her the first week on the job."

It had occurred to Mia more than once how much she could have benefited from a green-haired librarian in the small Nebraska town where she'd grown up. Not until she was well into adulthood did she realize that not all librarians were employed to scare children, like the dreaded circulation director at Cedar Ridge Municipal Branch with the spidery braid and hairy mole. Mia had cowered behind the legs of her father when he would stop in to check out a Neil Diamond CD or the latest release by Louis L'Amour. The moled woman had snapped at Mia once when she'd fingered a book on a stand, announcing down her nose that the book of Mia's interest was for display only and could not be checked out. Never mind that *Bird Calls of the Northeast* had not exactly beckoned to eight-year-old Mia anyway, but the chastisement was enough to keep books at an arm's length for years. How different Mia's interest in reading could have been had a spitfire like Frankie been the one behind the desk!

Frankie's supervisor, Ms. Nachtmusik, with her impossible surname that changed with each conversation, didn't know the gift Frankie was to her patrons.

"Hello, ladies." Gerry looked over his glasses. He stopped pecking madly at a calculator on the front counter. "How are things with you?"

"Mia's sick, Gerry." Frankie patted Mia on the head. "We need sick stuff."

Gerry pushed back on his stool and stood. He clucked like an unusually tall occupant of a henhouse. "Sick, Miss Mia? Headache? Stomach? Fever?"

Mia shook her head. "Stomach, I guess. I think crackers will be enough."

Gerry looked disgusted. "This is not your duty to decide. Miss Frankie and I will take care of the illness. Sit." He pointed to his stool and waved at her impatiently when she didn't jump at his command. Gerry shuffled off, muttering about the tragedy of young people living in cities without their parents.

Mia slipped Frankie a rolled-up reusable shopping bag and whispered, "Make sure to steer him away from pesticides." Frankie winked at Mia and skipped behind the man on his mission.

Mia greeted the next few patrons entering the store. She tried watching the game show on Gerry's small black-and-white, but she couldn't seem to follow the rules. *I'll just lay my head here for a moment*, she thought, pushing Gerry's calculator aside.

✦ ✦ ✦

"Oh, good heavenly gracious, we need to call an ambulance!" Gerry's words seeped like molasses through Mia's subconscious. She wondered who was injured and if it had anything to do with the impossible rules on that game show.

"Mia, honey, are you okay?" Frankie was tugging on her shoulder.

"Hmm?" Mia pulled her eyelids open into the glare of fluorescent lights. Her head was, indeed, on the front counter, but so was the rest of her body. She turned her head slowly to face Frankie, who had crouched down beside her and was inches from her face. "I'm lying on the conveyer belt."

"Yes, yes, you are," Frankie said while guiding Mia to a sitting position. She gauged her tone of voice to fit a three-year-old on Sudafed. "Gerry and I left to get some groceries and when we returned," she enunciated, "you were lying on the counter." She nodded up and down, up and down.

Mia shook her head. "I was really tired. I needed to sleep." Her voice trailed off. She kept her hands on her face for a moment, fingers brushing past a stud in her right nostril and the ring in her eyebrow. Eyes open, she peeked through the cracks in her fingers. Behind Gerry, who was patting his pockets frantically for cigarettes that hadn't been there since he'd quit a decade before, stood his son, Adam. Mia tried running her fi ngers through her yoga-tangle of hair.

Adam cleared his throat and smiled.

Mia realized she'd dropped her hands and had commenced a creepy stare session. "Hi, Adam," she said too loudly. "How are you?"

Adam bit his cheek in an attempt to take seriously a question coming from a woman sprawled next to a cash register. "I'm great, Mia. You?"

"Fantastic," she said and swung her legs to the side of her perch. Gerry rushed forward to offer her his arm, Adam close behind. Mia held up her hands in protest. "I'm fine, really," she said. "Just a little tired, apparently." She walked slowly to the front door and turned to wave. "Thanks, Gerry. You're a great host. Adam, good to see you. Frankie, are you ready?" She opened the door without waiting for a response and stepped out onto the sidewalk.

Gerry pushed away Frankie's twenty-dollar bill and handed her the sack of sick stuff as she fell in behind her friend.

✦   ✦   ✦

They walked five minutes in silence. Dusk was long gone, the sun having set early in the February evening. Mia was from the Midwest and didn't much mind Chicago winters; Frankie, however, hailed from Southern California and moaned every few steps as wind from the lake found its way through coats and mittens and headed straight for skin.

"I will never know why we have chosen this misery." Frankie held Mia at the crook of her arm like a geriatric patient. Mia felt too exhausted to protest. At the foot of the stairs leading to her apartment building, she stopped. She watched a dapper older gentleman with mocha skin descend the steps and allow his eyes to fall on her.

"Hey, Silas," she said.

"Evening, girls," Silas said. He dropped his keys in the side pocket of his suit and tipped his hat, a soft brown fedora trimmed in striped black ribbon. He cocked his head slightly and narrowed his gaze at Mia. "Girl, you don't look so hot." Silas furrowed his brow and looked at Frankie. "What's the story, Francesca?"

"We're not sure," Frankie said. "But don't worry. I'm taking her straight upstairs before she can toss her cookies again."

Silas took a nimble step back, sidestepping puddles in his retreat. "Honey, I'm sorry. Ain't no fun getting sick."

"Thanks," Mia said. She handed him a box of Lorna Doones from her stash of groceries. "Brought your favorites. Goodness knows I won't be needing a visit with Miss Lorna this evening," she said, wrinkling her nose at the thought.

Silas clucked and shook his head. "Your mama raised you right. I thank God for you, Mia, and I know my dear Bonnie is happy to look down from glory and see me so well taken care of." He patted her gloved hand. "I couldn't ask for a better neighbor. You get better now, you hear?"

The girls took the steps slowly. When they reached the front door and waited for Mia to fish keys out of her bag, Frankie cleared her throat.

"So, um, what was that business at Gerry's all about?"

Mia shook her head. She dug deeper in her purse. "This is one bizarre virus. I don't even remember making the decision to go to sleep."

"Yes, right. I didn't mean the counter episode. I meant the eye-lock with Gerry's son."

"Found them," Mia said and pushed her key into the lock. "Sorry, what were you saying?"

"Hair-fixing, googly-eye thing with Fig Leaf."

Mia tried to look disapproving. "You and your nicknames. I like the name Adam. I cringe to think of what you call me behind my back."

"Hmm," Frankie said. "Today would be a toss-up between Vomitronica and Queen of Feigned Emotional Distancing."

"I'm not feigning anything, for those of us who've read too much Jane Austen," Mia said. She led the way into the lobby elevator and pushed the button for the fourth floor. The door closed with a shudder and Mia shrugged. "It's really nothing."

Frankie crossed her arms and positioned her finger above the emergency stop button.

"All right." Mia sighed. "When I first moved to my apartment, I was momentarily single and also in need of a neighborhood grocery. I found Gerry's, and Adam was always there with his perfect smile and impeccable Persian manners." She sighed and watched the numbers light up on their ascent.

"Oh, my gosh. This is so *Rear Window*."

"Isn't that the one where the woman is paralyzed?"

"No," Frankie said with labored patience. "That's *An Affair to Remember*. I'm hinting less at paralysis, more at love at first sight."

Mia rolled her eyes as the elevator door opened. "I noticed

him, he noticed me, we flirted, and then I was no longer single."
Mia stepped into the hallway. "It was nothing. Seriously. As you
might remember, I'm happily in love with another man. End of
story." She led the way to her apartment door. "Sorry to disap-
point. I *was* recovering from an episode, remember."

"Exactly!" Frankie was triumphant. "Your defenses were
down, you were caught off guard and didn't have time to censor
what was and wasn't socially appropriate—"

"Shh. He might be home." Mia paused at her apartment
door and ignored Frankie's dramatic jab of her finger down her
throat.

"That would be *so* unusual," Frankie said, *sotto voce.* "You
can't mean he would be eating your food and smashing organic
potato chips under his rear as he watches *Baywatch* reruns on
your couch?"

Mia called into the room, "Anybody here?"

Frankie muttered, "Because we wouldn't expect you to be
anywhere else."

Mia pinched Frankie's arm when she heard rustling in the
living room. "Lars?"

He stepped into the entryway, blond hair tousled, mouth
opened in a wide yawn. "Hey, babe," he said around his yawn.
"Hey, Frankie."

"Hi, Lars," Frankie said sweetly. Mia avoided eye contact
with her friend and instead pulled her arms around Lars and
gave him her cheek to kiss.

"Don't exchange any of my germs," she said. "I think I'm
sick."

Lars stepped back, nudging Mia out of the embrace. "Really?" He wrinkled his nose. "Like puking sick?"

Mia unbuttoned her coat. Frankie tugged her friend's arms

out of the sleeves and unwrapped her from a bulky crocheted scarf. "Like, *totally* puking sick," she said, watching Lars for any recognition of her mocking tone. None detected, she rambled on. "She, like, ralphed after yoga and then at Gerry's she *totally* fell asleep under the scanner."

Lars had turned and was heading for the fridge. Mia shot a pleading look at Frankie, who sighed and nodded a momentary truce.

"You should have called and told me you were going to the store. We're almost out of soy milk," he said, nose in the fridge. "And I ate the last Carob Joy after lunch."

Mia filled a glass with water. Lars had piled his dishes in the sink, and it occurred to her to thank him, as this was a marked improvement from fi nding them all over the apartment, crusty, molding, and sometimes neglected until they smelled of rot. Determined not to conjure up any more detail of those images and too tired to explain to Frankie later why dirty dishes piled in the sink was a step upward, she sipped her water and shuffled toward the bedroom.

"Thanks, Frankie, for taking care of me," she said. "I owe you. But I can't think about it right now, okay?"

Frankie followed her into the bedroom. She turned the covers down as Mia undressed and placed a saucer of crackers on the bedside table. "You take care of yourself, do you hear me?" For a woman with blue hair, Frankie could command the maternal authority of Olivia Walton when summoned. "Call me tomorrow morning. Or before if you need me. Not that Lars isn't the nurturing, restorative type ..."

Mia moaned. She lowered herself into bed and curled up into a fetal position.

"All right, all right." Frankie spoke softly. She turned out the light. "Sleep well, Mimi." She waited a moment for an answer from under the down comforter but Mia was already drifting toward sleep.

2

THE SYSTEM

When Mia woke, inky black had settled in the room. She raised herself up on one elbow and made her eyes focus on the dresser clock. Nine twenty-four. She'd slept for two and a half hours. She kicked off the covers and was pleased the action didn't make her want to run to the restroom. Her fuzzy slippers peeked out from under the bed. They murmured a soft-shoe on the wood as she padded out to the living room. Lars was reading in the papasan chair by the window. The open pages of his book shone unnaturally in the only light illuminating the room. He looked up.

"How's your tummy?" he said, shutting his book. He stood and led her to the couch where they could sit together.

"Better," Mia said. She yawned. "I'm still really tired, but I think I'm hungry."

Lars pulled a soft green blanket from the back of the couch and draped it around Mia's lap and legs. "How about some pho? I stopped at Hanoi Market for some noodles."

Mia closed her eyes and smiled. "Perfect."

She let her head rest on a pillow while Lars heated her dinner in the kitchen. *See?* she told an internal Frankie. *This is how he is, not the mooch you think you see in him.*

When Mia closed her eyes, she could see Lars when they'd first met. They'd registered for the same senior seminar their final semester of college, "Patriarchy, Famine, and Genocide in Twenty-First-Century Africa." Seven students and one prof met weekly to discuss painfully long and depressing research articles on the state of African politics, economy, geography, and sociology. Mia had noticed Lars for his thoughtful comments, or at least that's how she told the story now. She left out that she first was drawn to Lars because of his lips. They were full, always pink, and seemed to encourage mind-wandering. The thought still made her blush, as she was not typically one to objectify men, certainly not while intending to concentrate on the effects of tribal patriarchy on modern African elections. But the lips were what got her attention. The thoughtful comments were just an excuse to watch the lips move.

"Here we go," Lars said. He set a steaming bowl of soup on the coffee table and tugged the table toward the couch. "Hold on," he said and returned to the kitchen. Mia could hear him rummaging around in a paper bag. He turned slowly into the family room, brow furrowed with the task of holding a wide mug of tea, chopsticks, and a saucer dotted with slices of lime.

"Such great service in this place," Mia said, laying her head on Lars's shoulder when he settled into the couch. "I should definitely eat here more often."

Lars kissed the top of Mia's dark curls. "I'm happy you're happy. My dad would so not believe how enlightened I am, male partner serving female and all that. You're one lucky girl, you know?"

Mia could hear the smile in Lars's voice and tried her best to exude her luckiness. "Absolutely I do. Neither of my parents was very good at the partnership thing either, so we're both rene-gades." Her first slurp of broth sank, one pampering centimeter after another, down her throat and into her body. She hummed her approval.

"Good?" Lars said. He rose from the couch to snap up his cell phone, which was trumpeting a wild dance tune by his favorite world music group, HealPeace. He checked to see who was calling and shut the ringer off. "Bryan," he said to himself.

"Really?" Mia squeezed a lime wedge over her soup. "That's great. Does he need you for a job?" She cleared her throat after the question, regretting how eager she'd sounded.

"Probably," Lars muttered. He scrolled through a text message. "I'm kind of busy, though, so I don't know if it will work out."

Mia kept her eyes on her noodles. When asked about his profession, Lars said he was a freelance writer. This translated mostly to the odd short piece here and there, usually contracted by Lars's high-school buddy, Bryan, a magazine editor who was kind enough to pass along work when it was available. Th e relationship was tenuous, as Lars felt Bryan stifled his creative spirit with the extensive editing he did on each piece before publication. Mia had seen some of Lars's rough work, however, and felt Bryan was a literary savior. *Irregardless* and *satisfication*, for example, were not the best ways to use the English language, try as Lars might to convince. Neither was opening a piece with a two-hundred-word quotation by Engels a foolproof device to engage the reader.

"You're too busy?" Mia asked. "What are you so busy with?"

Lars looked up from his phone. "Did I pay half our rent this month?"

"Yes," Mia said. She avoided his gaze by the tip of her mug.

"And the three months before that?"

"Yes, you did," Mia said. She groaned into her tea, the voice of her mother admonishing her (again) for having a "live-in" outside the bounds of marriage.

"What's to gain?" her mother would say in her best Dr. Laura voice. "Why *should* he propose when he has all the benefits without the risk?"

Not that Mia's mom was one to talk about marital success, Mia tried to remind herself. But eighteen years of brainwashing had to have repercussions on a girl's thought life.

"Okay, then," Lars said, tossing his phone onto the chair by the window. "You can feel confident that my decision not to work will not adversely affect our *arrangement*." He strode back toward the kitchen and Mia let him go. She could barely keep her eyes open and was finding it increasingly difficult to enjoy the act of eating. This left little reserve for entering into an argument with Lars. Lars, who could crush an otherwise bright person in a debate. Lars, whose tenacity wearied Mia to the point that she was always the first to forget the original point of discussion and the first to give up and give in. Having witnessed many of these "conversations," Frankie had developed a disgust for what she saw as Lars's unwillingness to lose a battle.

"Stop letting him do that!" she would say to Mia later. "He is not always right." Mia would shrug. "I know, and he probably does, too, on some level. But it's so much easier to let those things go. I just don't care enough and he does, so we both come out ahead, right?"

Mia shuffled to the kitchen. She covered her bowl with plastic wrap and put the leftovers in the fridge. On her way out of the room, she met Lars in the hallway near the front door. He was pulling on his coat.

"I'm meeting Dan at the Dive. He needs a little cheering up."

Mia leaned against the door frame. "What's wrong? Something with Avery?"

Lars snorted. "You could say that. She's threatening to dump him if they don't get engaged."

Mia nodded slowly. "An interesting way to resolve the marriage question. Spend the rest of your lives together or dump each other. It seems like there should be some middle ground there, doesn't it?"

Lars moved to her and enveloped her in his arms. "See? That's exactly why I'm with you and not someone like Avery. You acknowledge the ridiculousness of convention. You see through marriage as an antiquated system left over from—"

"—the unequal and barbaric days of class wars, dowries, and institutionalized sexism." Mia looked up and smiled. "I agree completely."

He kissed her. "I know. And knowing that makes me risk getting your plague by kissing your lips." He kissed her again. "You rest. Don't wait up." He turned and locked the door on his way out.

He hadn't apologized, but Mia thought there must be lots of ways to communicate one was sorry, and maybe not always with a penance of words.

✦ ✦ ✦

A week later Mia sat with her head in her hands. Her desk phone was ringing and she was summoning the strength to answer it. "Urban Hope," she said, resting her forehead in her palm.

"You sound horrible. Are you still feeling like excrement?"

Frankie's voice was inappropriately loud but there was no volume control on Mia's ancient phone.

"I would appreciate you not mentioning anything remotely related to an unpleasant image, smell, or taste. I cannot be held accountable with what I might do with such information." Mia swiveled in her chair and leaned her head against her office window. She told herself the cool of the glass was soothing.

"Have you gone to the doctor yet?"

"Not exactly."

"Mia, this is your big chance to stick it to the Man, just like you and Lars connive to do. You work for the system, the system is broken, the system pays peanuts and keeps the downtrodden down while the wealthy thrive. *But* the system gives great insurance benefits, so get your rear to the doctor's office and start cashing in, for once."

"Are you chewing on something?" Mia watched a little girl cross the alley below, holding with a death grip to the fingers of her father.

Even from two stories up, Mia could see the red patent leather shine on the girl's shoes.

"Yep," Frankie said, "and it is so stinking good. I've always wondered what those lamb things taste like. You know, those cute kabobs impaled on their little skewers at that place on Fullerton?"

Mia groaned. "All right. I'll make an appointment with a doctor."

"Excellent," Frankie said, so loudly that Mia had to pull the phone away from her ear. "Tell them it's an emergency and that you work for the government. Maybe they'll squeeze you in this afternoon."

"You have definitely inflated my job to mean something it

doesn't."

"Love ya, kid. Call me later."

Mia let the phone drop to its cradle. She pulled up Google and set about searching for a board-certified answer to her problem.